A Grave

Issue

A Grave Issue

A FUNERAL PARLOR MYSTERY

Lillian Bell

CROOKED
LANE

NEW YORK

Copyright © 2018 by The Quick Brown Fox & Company LLC.

Published in the United States by Crooked Lane Books, an imprint of The Quick Brown Fox & Company LLC.

Crooked Lane Books and its logo are trademarks of The Quick Brown Fox & Company LLC.

Library of Congress Catalog-in-Publication data available upon request.

ISBN (paperback): 978-1-68331-725-8
ISBN (hardcover): 978-1-68331-490-5
ISBN (ePub): 978-1-68331-491-2
ISBN (ePDF): 978-1-68331-492-9

Cover illustration by Ben Perini
Book design by Jennifer Canzone

Printed in the United States.

www.crookedlanebooks.com

Crooked Lane Books
34 West 27th St., 10th Floor
New York, NY 10001

Hardcover Edition: February 2018
Paperback Edition: August 2018

10 9 8 7 6 5 4 3 2 1

Chapter One

The Verbena Free Press

THURSDAY, JULY 5

Emu Death Possibly Caused by Foul Play

Animal Control and the Verbena Police have been investigating the unexpected passing of Rosemarie and Alan Brewer's pet emu, Vincent. Ms. Brewer has blamed her neighbors Kyle and Lola Hansen for the death. Ms. Brewer claims that Vincent was in good health until the Hansen's two dogs barked at the bird and frightened Vincent enough to run in circles until he collapsed on the ground. "Those vicious attack dogs scared Vincent to death," Ms. Brewer said. "Who will they kill next? None of us are safe."

Representatives from Animal Control and the Verbena Police Department have stated that they can find no causal relationship between the dogs barking and the death of the emu. In addition, there is nothing illegal about Kyle and Lola Hansen's dogs. Emilio Fuentes of Animal Control told the *Free Press* that there was no evidence that the Hansens'

1

dogs were vicious. "Even if they were," Fuentes said, "they're kept fenced in and pose no danger to anyone."

Detective Butler of the Verbena Police Department stated that no laws had been broken and that he would not be pursuing the matter any further.

D ead bodies are nothing new to me. I grew up in a funeral home. I was taken straight from the nursery at Verbena Memorial Hospital to the top floor of the Turner Family Funeral Home, where I lived until I was eighteen years old. At which point I hightailed it out of here as if snapping packs of jackals were on my heels. But still, having a dead body around was the norm. They didn't scare me. They didn't gross me out. They honestly didn't interest me that much.

Murdered bodies, though? Murdered bodies were a whole different thing. Even after covering the police beat in Los Angeles and being on the scene of dozens of shootings and stabbings, murdered bodies still shocked me, and they definitely interested me. There was always a story when there was a murder. Always. And I loved stories. You don't become a journalist if you're not interested in stories.

Nate Johar, Pluma Vista County medical examiner, had brought the body in, zipped up in one of those black body bags, and had wheeled him directly into the embalming room where he'd be conducting the autopsy. Pluma Vista

2

County, home to Verbena, which was, in turn, home to the Turner Family Funeral Home, wasn't a big place. We were near big places. Sacramento wasn't that far. Neither was San Francisco. Napa was a day trip. On our own, though? We were pretty small, mainly the unwanted corners of a few other counties, the sweepings left on the cutting-room floor after gerrymandering. Because we were small, we didn't have the resources to have a dedicated office for our medical examiner. It's not that uncommon. In small places and a lot of rural places, the medical examiner generally works out of funeral homes. The honor rotates. And by "honor," I mean total and complete pain in the ass.

I had decided to hover nearby for a number of reasons. I wanted to be around in case he needed anything. Uncle Joey was out picking someone up, and I wanted Nate out of our embalming room as soon as possible so Uncle Joey's workflow wouldn't be disrupted. Also, it was the first time I'd seen Nate since I'd come home. Circumstances—I'm being kind to myself here—had brought me back home ten years after I left, my tail quite firmly between my legs and having eaten so much crow that I'd be picking feathers from between my teeth for years to come. Nate had come home by choice to take over the medical examiner's position when old Dr. Pittman retired. His tail could fly high, and I didn't think he'd eaten a single bite of crow.

From where I sat at my uncle's desk in the basement, I couldn't see anything, but I could hear everything.

Nate said, "Subject is a forty-eight-year-old white male identified as Alan Brewer. Cause of death at the moment appears to be a bullet wound in his forehead."

I sat up straight in my chair and swallowed a gasp. I didn't want Nate to know I was eavesdropping so I needed to be quiet. It was shocking, though. Alan Brewer, manager of the Verbena Union Bank, vice president of the Downtown Verbena Business Association, member of the Verbena Chamber of Commerce, lay dead of a bullet to the forehead only a few feet away from me. I'd known right then that it was the emu's fault. We'd all known that bird was bad news, but I didn't think anyone could have predicted how bad it would get. I certainly wouldn't have guessed in a million years that things could go so horribly wrong because of a bird that couldn't even fly.

* * *

A while later, Nate came out of the embalming room, drying his hands. "All done," he said.

"Are you releasing the body for burial?" Sometimes the medical examiner held on to people for a while until everything was resolved.

"Not quite yet." He gestured to his case. "I took some samples. We'll run tox screens and all the rest, but it's pretty clear what happened."

"Is it . . . homicide?" I asked.

Nate looked at me and didn't answer.

I held up my hands. "Right. Right. I get it. You can't say anything." Except sometimes the things people didn't say were a lot louder than what actually came out of their mouths. "I'll take it from here," I said. I'd find out later from Uncle Joey where Alan would be going. For now, he could stay in our refrigeration unit at the back of the basement.

"Thanks." He stopped and rubbed the back of his neck. "Thanks for this, and thanks for the use of your facility."

I stood to walk him to the door. "That last part isn't exactly at our discretion."

He smiled. It made him look younger, more like the Nate I'd known back in high school, back when we'd been boyfriend and girlfriend, back when we'd thought we'd be together forever, back before we'd gone to different schools and taken different paths. "I know, but some places make that clearer than others."

At the door, he stopped. He'd always been taller than me, but I was even more aware of it now, standing close with my nose at about the same level as his Adam's apple. There was an awkward pause, and the air seemed to warm around us. Then he stuck out his hand. "It was nice to see you, Desiree."

I shook his hand, feeling oddly deflated. "Ditto."

I leaned against the door and watched him go, just like I'd watched him drive away dozens of times when we'd been kids. Well, not kids. At least, we hadn't thought we were kids back then. We'd thought we were all kinds of things. We'd thought we were going to conquer the world. We thought we could make our dreams into reality through sheer force of will. We'd thought we were in love.

I sighed and went into the embalming room to get Alan. Nate had taken the black body bag with him and had left Alan covered by a sheet. Damn. He was on the old gurney, the one with the sticky wheel. I'd been meaning to go after it with some WD-40 but hadn't gotten to it. Whatever. If I took a bit of a running start, I should be able to get it over the door sill and straight back to the refrigeration unit.

I got behind the gurney, pulled it back toward myself, and went for it. We made it over the sill, but not in a straight line, and I banged it a little against the doorframe as we went through. The sheet that Nate had draped over Alan slipped.

There he was. Alan Brewer. In all his glory. Well, not all his glory. His lower half was still under the sheet. It was hard to take my eyes away from that bullet hole, truly right in the center of his forehead. As precisely placed as a bull's-eye on a target. I reached to pull the sheet back up over him, which is when I realized that his chest was also exposed along with a great big hickey right over his left nipple. Apparently Alan went out with a spring his step. Lucky him. Well, I supposed the bullet to the forehead outweighed a night of passion that would produce a hickey like that one on the lucky scale. I pulled the sheet up and wheeled him to the refrigeration unit.

Alan Brewer. Bullet wound to the forehead. Unless he slipped in the shower and fell on a bullet in just the wrong way to jam it into his forehead, this was going to be foul play. Or should I say *fowl* play?

Chapter Two

The Verbena Free Press

SATURDAY, JULY 13

Local Businessman Murdered

Alan Brewer, manager of the Verbena Union Bank, was found shot to death on his property at approximately seven AM on Friday morning. Mr. Brewer's wife, Rosemarie, realized that he had not returned from collecting eggs from the couple's chicken coop after she took her shower. She went to investigate and found Mr. Brewer dead from a gunshot wound to the forehead. "Whoever did this is a monster!" Ms. Brewer said. "They could have hit the chickens, too."

Detective Butler of the Verbena Police Department has said that they are following several leads but declined to comment on the identities of any individual suspects. "We're looking at everybody and everything," he said.

Two days before the murder, Ms. Brewer had been in an altercation at the Turner Family Funeral Home with neighbor Lola Hansen. Detective Butler would neither deny nor confirm whether that altercation was related to the current situation. Ms. Brewer and Ms. Hansen both declined to be interviewed.

Mr. Brewer was taken to the Turner Family Funeral Home. Desiree Turner, assistant funeral director, was also a witness to the altercation between Ms. Brewer and Ms. Hansen. She declined to comment on that issue. Mr. Brewer's murder is the first to have taken place in Verbena since Ms. Turner's return to Verbena.

It was two days after I'd wheeled Alan into our refrigeration unit when Henrietta Lambert's cell phone went off just as Uncle Joey wheeled Mr. Murray out of the Lilac Room to the back entrance of Turner Family Funeral Home, where he would be loaded into the hearse and transported to the Lawn of Heaven Cemetery. I shot Henrietta what I hoped was a death glare. She had the good grace to blush. Silencing your phone during a funeral was just good manners, and Henrietta had been to enough services to know better. Henrietta was one of our regulars. Olive Wheeler, Henrietta Lambert, and Grace Cohen attended most of the funerals that took place here at the funeral home, nearly all the funerals held at the Church of Open Fields on Oriole Street, and a healthy smattering of the ones at Beth Chaverim on Robin Avenue. Other women watched soap operas or knit. Olive, Henrietta, and Grace attended funeral services.

I didn't care that Mr. Murray only had seven family members there (one daughter, one son-in-law, three grandchildren, two nieces), that the service was basically over (a few words from Pastor Campbell, a cute memory from the son-in-law about meeting Mr. Murray for the first time, a recitation of the twenty-first psalm), or that Mr. Murray's daughter had picked our most stripped-down funeral package (basic casket with no drape, no memory box, and no decorative accessories; twenty-five printed programs; funeral in the Lilac Room; transportation to the cemetery, but no video montage, no music, no frill and no fuss). Silencing your cell phone was a matter of respect.

I brought Henrietta's walker over to her from where it was resting against the wall. She started fishing through the pocket of the walker for her phone before I could say anything. "Sorry," she said. "I swear I thought I'd turned it off."

"No cookies?" Olive asked.

"The family's having a postfuneral reception at their home," I said as I brought her walker from where I'd stashed it against the wall.

She sniffed. "Doesn't seem like much of a celebration of life."

"Because he lived too long," Grace said. "He took too long, and now they're giving him the bum's rush out the door."

"I'm sure they're very sad," I said, delivering another walker. I felt a little bad. I'd been the one to convince

Sheena Murray that she could have a small gathering at her home and not do a big thing here. She'd looked so exhausted when she'd come in to make the arrangements. I almost offered to clean her house for her before people came over. Now Grace, Olive, and Henrietta—sitting where they always sat looking like three gray-haired Fates—were throwing shade over it. "Sheena's really exhausted. I think we should cut her some slack."

Grace shot me a look through her coke-bottle-thick glasses. "This is Olive's walker. It's got her name right here." She pointed to a piece of tape that did indeed have Olive's name on it. "Your father always knew which walker was which."

"Sorry," I said and handed it to Olive, who patted my hand.

"They didn't look too sad," Grace called after me. "You look sadder than they did."

"I'm sad," Olive said. "I wanted a cookie. I mean, why bother with a funeral at all if you're not going to at least offer people cookies?"

It was one of those existential questions that simply did not have an answer.

Henrietta held her phone as far from her face as her arm would allow. "I can't read this. I think it's a news alert from the *Free Press*, but it's blurry. Can you read it? Don't make me find my reading glasses." She shoved the phone at me.

I decided not to mention that her reading glasses were hanging from a chain around her neck, because I was curious too. What was Rafe Valdez up to now? And when had the *Verbena Free Press* gotten so high tech that they sent out news alerts? Whatever it was, I'd better not be in the article. I'd shown up in a few too many already, and my family was none too happy about that. I read the message on Henrietta's phone and gasped. I thought about asking to borrow her glasses to be sure I'd read it right.

"Well, what is it?" Henrietta asked. She thumped her walker on the floor for emphasis.

Not believing the words that were coming out of my mouth, I said, "Kyle Hansen has been arrested for the murder of Alan Brewer. Can you ladies let yourselves out?"

I didn't wait for an answer. I ran.

* * *

Verbena, California, is no place to be running around in panty hose and heels during the summer. I remembered that the second I stepped out of the nicely chilled interior of Turner Family Funeral Home and into the furnace that was my hometown. It felt like I'd hit an actual wall of heat. Verbena is nestled into the upper corners of the Central Valley. People grow things here. Tomatoes.

Corn. Almonds. Families. Summers were hot and dry during the day with plenty of times that the temperature soared over one hundred degrees. Today was one of those days. The inside of my mouth went dry the second I hit the outside air. I shaded my eyes from the unrelenting glare of the sun with my hand.

My dry mouth and stinging eyes didn't matter, though. Kyle had been arrested. Kyle, the man who had practically been my second father as I'd grown up, who couldn't and wouldn't be unkind or cruel to anyone, even Alan Brewer, whom he had plenty of reasons to be unkind and cruel to. I had to find Lola and see what I could do to help. If Kyle had been arrested, I was pretty sure I knew where he'd be and therefore where Lola would be: the police station.

I made it downtown and squeezed my dad's black Honda Element into a parking space before the air conditioning in the car even had time to take effect. I raced into the police station while trying to stop the back of my skirt from sticking to my legs. I skidded to a stop in front of Lola, who was sitting in one of the hard plastic chairs in the lobby and staring straight ahead with her jaw a little slack, her normally mirror-smooth hair uncombed.

Rafe Valdez, editor and publisher of the *Verbena Free Press*, was two steps away from Lola, notepad in hand. I positioned myself between Rafe and Lola. "Ms. Hansen has no comment."

He smiled, white teeth a blinding flash. "I haven't asked her a question, Ms. Turner."

"Doesn't matter. She has no comment regardless." I crossed my arms over my chest.

"Are you sure she and her husband don't want to get their side of the story out there before the whole town makes up its mind?" He cocked his head to one side, and his dark hair flopped over his forehead. My fingers simultaneously itched to brush it off his face and to punch him.

"You know that this is at least partly your fault, don't you?" I asked.

He touched his fingers to his chest. "*Moi*? How could I be in any way responsible for a murder?"

I shook my head. He knew what he'd done. He might not have known what the consequences would be, but his stories on the escalating animosity between the two sets of neighbors had certainly not helped settle anything down. No, he'd whipped it all up into as much of a frenzy as he could. Then he'd kept the frenzy going whenever possible. But it would do me no good to argue with him, and more important, it would do Lola and Kyle no good. The less you said to a reporter, the better. I knew. I used to be one. "No. Comment."

"Fine." He reached into his pocket and pulled out a card, which he reached around me to hand to Lola. "Call me if you change your mind."

"She won't." I crossed my arms over my chest and glared. It probably wasn't that impressive. I'm only about five foot four and a touch on the scrawny side. Definitely not the good Viking stock of my Dad's family. My sister Donna got those genes.

I watched Rafe leave the building and then slipped into the chair next to her and took her hand. "Lola, what happened?"

Her head turned slowly toward me like a carnival puppet. "They arrested Kyle." Her tone was flat.

I rubbed her ice-cold hand to try to get some warmth back into it. My own were still nearly hot enough to cook with thanks to the steering wheel of the Element. Why had my dad always insisted on a black car? Wasn't that just a bit cliché? "I know that part, but why?"

"The emu." A tear leaked down her cheek. "The emu and the gun. The stupid gun." She took her hand from mine and wrapped her arms around her middle as if her stomach hurt.

I didn't understand what she was saying. "What gun? Whose gun?"

"Our gun. They're saying it's the one that killed Alan. It couldn't be, but when we went to look for it in the gun safe—the one on the porch—it was gone." She began to rock in her chair. "They found it in the pond down by Rosemarie's chicken coop, down where . . . it happened. Somebody threw it in there."

While murder didn't happen much in Verbena, it was pretty common in Los Angeles. I'd covered plenty of murders as I'd worked my way up through the reporting ranks in the six years I'd lived there. "The gun is the only evidence they have?" I asked. Guns were stolen all the time. A name on the registration didn't mean that person had shot the gun. It didn't even mean the gun was in their possession.

Lola nodded. "When Luke arrested Kyle, he said Kyle shouldn't have used his own gun, or he should have done a better job of disposing of it."

"Luke? Luke Butler is the arresting officer?" A glowing ember of anger started to burn through the haze and confusion of the news of Kyle's arrest.

Lola put her face in her hands. "Yes. Luke Butler. And to think I gave that boy an A in Yearbook."

I made a noise in the back of my throat. "We'll see about this." I marched up to the desk where a female officer sat. I'd seen her before but didn't know her name. "I need to speak to Luke Butler immediately. Tell him it's Desiree Turner."

"I know who you are. You're the funeral parlor lady." She picked up the phone. "Butler, Desiree Turner's asking to see you."

I leaned forward to speak into the phone's receiver. "Demanding. Demanding to see you."

The officer straight-armed me away and glared. She listened for a second and then hung up. "He'll be right out."

I nodded and stepped back. I glanced over my shoulder at Lola, who was looking smaller by the moment. It broke my heart. I felt an almost physical pain at seeing her so diminished.

Then Luke stepped into the lobby. He was a good-looking man, if you liked that all-American-boy kind of thing with the blond hair, blue eyes, and freckles. If you went for the whole broad-shouldered thing, he was okay, I guessed. He hadn't made me wait. I was a little surprised but gave him points for not playing games.

"Hello, Death Ray," he said, using the nickname he'd saddled me with back in grade school.

And just like that, he was back to zero points. "Hello, Luke. I need to talk to you about Kyle Hansen."

He sighed. "I figured. Come on back." He gestured for me to follow him through the double doors. He ushered me into an interrogation room and shut the door. I started to protest. He raised a hand to stop me. "It's so we can speak privately. There's not much of that out there." He gestured to the open room dotted with cubicles. Verbena's police and fire department were housed in the same building and had been since the town rebuilt after the fire of 1913. It was a great building, with light-colored brick with high arches for the fire trucks and decorative clay tiles all around. The exterior spoke of solidity and calm authority.

Inside it spoke more to a twenty-first-century population, with technology crammed into a more than one-hundred-year-old space and cords and wires and cubicles everywhere.

I sat back in my chair. "What possible reason could you have for arresting Kyle Hansen for Alan Brewer's murder?"

He made a face. "I assumed you'd spoken to Lola already. It was Kyle's gun that shot Alan."

"His gun, but not him," I countered.

"His gun, his motive, his opportunity." He ticked the items off on his fingers. "Look, I've spent some time studying homicides. The ones that take place between neighbors generally have two things in common: guns and dogs. There's pretty much always a dog and definitely always a gun. We've got the same thing here. Dogs and guns." He paused. "And, of course, the emu."

"You really think Kyle would kill someone over an emu-related dispute?" I scoffed. The whole idea was ridiculous. Anyone who knew Kyle at all could surely see that.

"That may have been where it started, but you know it had grown bigger than that. You were there when Rosemarie and Lola got into that fistfight." He pointed his finger at me like I was somehow responsible.

Because I was responsible, in a way. I shifted in my seat. If only I'd been able to stop that fight. It had happened at Delia Burns's funeral service. Delia had never hurt a soul in her life. She died in her bed of what my grandfather used to call "the blessed heart attack." She'd turned eighty-seven two months before, lived on her own, and still had all her teeth. Then one Thursday morning, she simply hadn't woken up. When Cheryl Cooper stopped by with some coffee cake and no one answered the door, she let herself in with the spare key Delia kept under a flower pot. She found Delia in bed with the blankets pulled up to her chin and wearing her special satin bonnet to maintain her perm until her next salon appointment at Cut 'n' Curl on Main Street.

The blessed heart attack had a special place in my grandfather's pantheon of deaths, and it was a vaunted one. I'd been happy for him when it had been the way he went in the end. I wondered what he would have thought about how his son, my dad, had gone.

Rosemarie had been seated in the third row at Delia's funeral, two seats in, quietly looking at her smartphone while pretending not to. I wasn't judging. If I could have been playing spider solitaire instead of standing by the big blown-up portrait of Delia and trying to smile the right amount of smile (warm and welcoming, but not having fun), I would totally have been doing it. Instead, I had to content myself with looking at the top of Rosemarie's head, where dark roots were starting to show along the part in her honey-blonde hair, and wondering if there was anything interesting happening on Facebook.

I didn't know Rosemarie. At least, not well. She hadn't even been Rosemarie Brewer (or a blonde) when I left town. She'd been Rosemarie Maldonado and a brunette back then. She'd been a big deal on the softball team back in the day. She'd had a changeup that would make your jaw drop. She also apparently had daddy issues that had led her to marry a man fifteen years her senior.

Then Lola Hansen walked in. Lola had been my journalism teacher at Verbena High back in the day. At the time, I'd thought of her as a sophisticated older woman. She'd been the same age I was now. I still thought she was sophisticated, with her dark hair cut in a smooth bob and wearing a beautifully cut sleeveless tunic over capri-length leggings and ballet flats. She was where everything started for me. She was the one who told me I could write. Plus her husband, Kyle Hansen, had been my dad's BFF. Lola and Kyle didn't have kids but had been two of the many people who stepped in after my mom died to help my dad parent Donna and me.

Lola and Kyle were two of the reasons I'd come back to Verbena. I'd called Lola when I didn't know what else to do, and she'd made it simple. "Come home," she'd said. "Take a breather, and we'll figure it out from there."

When she strode in that day, my professional assistant-to-the-funeral-director smile went from carefully maintained to genuinely warm.

"Desiree," she said, opening her arms.

Then I remembered Rosemarie and the emu.

Before I could do anything, before I could usher Lola out or distract Rosemarie or do one of those other sleight-of-hand moves my dad used to do to diffuse confrontation and unpleasantness before it started, Rosemarie had risen from her seat and strode up to Lola, fists clenched at her sides. "So you'll come to this funeral but not to Vincent's?" she asked, her voice tight.

Lola took a deep breath and schooled her features. "I'm sorry, Rosemarie. I didn't think it was appropriate—"

Rosemarie cut her off. "Why? Because you were responsible for his death?"

I stepped between them the way I'd seen my dad do dozens of times, quietly and smoothly. Death didn't always bring out the best in families and friends. Disputes arose, but Dad felt those disputes didn't need to mar a perfectly nice memorial service. He'd made it look easy. Dad had made pretty much everything look easy. He was that guy.

"Rosemarie, let's remember why we're here and focus on Miss Delia, okay?" I said, hands up in front of me to stop her advance.

Lola tried to move to the side, but Rosemarie shifted to continue to block her way. Lola sighed. "Excuse me, Rosemarie. I need to get to a seat."

"There's no 'excuse' for you, you murderer!" Rosemarie's voice rose on the last word, and everyone who hadn't been looking already—which I think was only Henrietta, and probably only because she needed to change the batteries in her hearing aids—swiveled around.

I moved a chair aside so I could stand between the two women again. "Let's sit down and talk about this later."

They both ignored me.

Lola looked down at Rosemarie. "Don't be ridiculous, Rosemarie. There was no murder." She tried to step around Rosemarie again.

Rosemarie moved to block Lola. "Then explain to me why Vincent is dead."

Lola sighed and shut her eyes for a second. I could practically hear her counting to ten. Lola said, "I'm sorry that Vincent died, but it still doesn't have anything to do with me. Maurice and Barry are farm dogs. They bark. If you let your emu run up and down the fence line like some kind of crazy bird-relay machine, it's going to get barked at. Besides, the barking might not have had anything to do with its death anyway. No one has proved that. Maybe it just had a heart attack. Birds die."

"It? You're calling Vincent an 'it'?" Rosemarie's voice had risen to a very high pitch, and two round splotches of red had appeared high on her cheekbones.

"It. He. Whatever. It was a bird. My dogs barked at it. It's dead. We've been over this, Rosemarie. With animal control. With the police. If you have anything else to say, please contact my lawyer. I know you received the cease-and-desist letter. I have the receipt on file." Lola looked over at me—finally—and gave me an eyebrow raise.

Rosemarie took a step forward, crowding Lola. Lola stepped back, but there was no more space; there was a chair behind her. The back of her knees hit it, and she toppled backward.

Lola shouted, "You pushed me! You all saw it! She pushed me! You've gone too far this time, Rosemarie. Too far!"

"Oh, shut your pie hole, you big whiner!" Rosemarie screamed back. "I never touched you. Just like your dogs never touched Vincent!" Then she nudged Lola with her toe. Well, nudged with purpose, let's say. It'd be hard to call it a kick, but it wasn't friendly.

Lola came up swinging.

I tried to pull them apart and got an elbow in the gut from Rosemarie for my trouble. When I saw Grace heading toward the melee with her walker as if she could break it up, I ran for the phone and dialed 9-1-1.

The newspaper coverage had been just this side of epic.

Chapter Three

The Verbena Free Press

THURSDAY, JULY 11

Female Fisticuffs at Funeral Home

Two Verbena women were arrested Friday afternoon on charges of disturbing the peace and assault and battery. Lola Hansen and Rosemarie Brewer were both attending the funeral of Miss Delia Burns (see obituary on page B4) when an argument began between the two women. The situation escalated quickly into a physical altercation. Witnesses say that while it was Ms. Brewer who made the first move by pushing Ms. Hansen backward over a chair, Ms. Hansen held her own in the scuffle and landed several sound punches. Police arrived before a definitive victor could be called.

Desiree Turner, assistant funeral director at Turner Family Funeral Home, declined to comment on the incident. Ms. Turner returned to her family business recently after

24

leaving her position as an on-air reporter for KLVX TV in Los Angeles. No other fistfights are on record as having occurred at the funeral home prior to her assumption of that position.

It had irritated my family; this was not the kind of press they wanted for Turner Family Funeral Home. It had come to the notice of the superintendent of schools who had notified Lola that her teaching contract could be nullified because of a morals clause that specifically forbade public fighting. And it had landed us here with Kyle arrested and Lola looking like she'd been run over by a whole herd of emus.

I squinted my eyes at Luke and leaned forward. "Kyle didn't do it."

"Desiree—"

I cut him off. "Do you have any other evidence?"

"That's not something I have to share with you." He crossed his arms over his chest.

"Did you even look at anyone else?" I knew a few things from my police beat days. I knew who usually committed murder. "Did you look at Rosemarie?"

"You don't think we looked at her? The spouse is the first person we look at. That's detective training 101. Have you seen her? She's been like a zombie since Alan was killed. She can barely put one foot in front of the other. She's grief-stricken. What about a motive for her?

And how did she get Kyle's gun? They lived next door, but they were only speaking to each other through lawsuits." He leaned back and shook his head. "No. It's Kyle. I'm sure of it."

I stood. "I'm sure it's not." He had a point about Rosemarie, though. I couldn't imagine leaving a love bite on someone's chest and then turning around and shooting him in the forehead.

"Then who?" he sneered.

That stopped me only for a second. "I'll figure it out, and then you'll see it isn't Kyle."

He stood and leaned onto the table between us on clenched fists. "Fine. Prove that it's not him, Death Ray."

"I will, Butler." I flung open the door of the interrogation room and stalked out. I marched out to the front lobby to find Janet Provost sitting next to Lola.

"Janet?" Janet Provost was the head of the PTA when I was in grade school. She was the mom in charge of first aid on every volleyball team that I'd been on with her daughter, Ruthie. She ran fundraisers and got us Band-Aids and constantly complained about her weight while simultaneously baking every week "for the kids."

"I came as soon as I saw the news alert." She stood to give me a hug. She wasn't much taller than me, but she was significantly more squishy. She smelled like vanilla. I didn't really want her to let me go. She pushed me back to arm's length anyway. "You look thin. I brought banana bread."

Sure enough there was a plate of banana bread covered with plastic wrap sitting on one of the chairs.

"Thanks, but why are you here?" I asked, not wanting to be rude but very much wanting to protect Lola from everyone, even if they brought banana bread.

She straightened. "I'm Lola and Kyle's lawyer. I've been representing them in their dispute with Rosemarie and Alan. As soon as I heard about Kyle's arrest, I came to help. They won't let me in to see him. They say they're processing him." She sniffed like she'd caught a whiff of something rotten.

I was still trying to catch up mentally. "You're a lawyer?"

"I went back to school when Ruthie left for college." She smiled. "Best decision I ever made. I love it."

Ruthie was my age. Let's say it took Janet three years to get through law school. That still left the whole passing-the-bar thing. "So you've been a lawyer for how long?"

"Two years now," Janet said.

Two years. Two years of experience. Kyle's life was on the line. Well, maybe not his life—California hasn't executed a prisoner since 2006—but his liberty was definitely up for grabs. "Janet, this is a murder case."

"I'm aware." She heaved a sigh. "Look, do you remember when the school board was going to cut funding for girls' volleyball?"

I did. The school board meeting had been a bloodbath. Janet had organized a protest, gotten a petition out and signed, and compiled a report showing how participating in sports could positively affect young women's lives. They hadn't cut the program and had actually ended up increasing our funding because of the public pressure she had generated. "I hadn't thought about that in ages."

"Well, think about it now. Think about the person who organized that in her free time, and now imagine her in a courtroom with a law degree." She raised her eyebrows.

I nodded slowly. "Okay, then. So what do we do now?"

"Now? Now you take Lola home, and I'll see what I can do here for Kyle. It may be a few days before there's a hearing, but I'll make sure they know we're watching them." She picked up the plate. "And you eat a piece of banana bread."

We said our good-byes, mine mumbled through crumbs, and I shepherded Lola out of the police station and tucked her into the passenger seat of my car. "I'm going to fix this, Lola."

I would too. I had to. I'd lost my father in the past year—I wasn't going to lose any of the father figures I had left, and I certainly wasn't going to lose this one to Luke-freaking-Butler.

* * *

I'd wanted to take Lola back to Turner's. I could take care of her there, but she'd shaken her head and said, "I can't. Maurice and Barry need me."

I sighed. I loved Maurice and Barry. There wasn't a better pair of Australian shepherds out there. They were the dogs in Luke's dogs-plus-emus-plus-guns-equals-dead-neighbors equation, though. I shrugged out of my suit jacket, positioned the AC to blow on my face, and headed out of town. Lola sunk down into the passenger seat, head pressed against the window. I reached over and patted her clenched hand. She whimpered. "What can I do?" I asked.

"I don't know," she said, a catch in her voice. "I just don't know."

I let go of her hand and focused on my driving as the road began to wind and twist through the walnut orchards and fields of tomatoes. You never knew when you were going to come around a curve to find a combine blocking the road. We finally pulled into the driveway of Lola and Kyle's place about four miles out of town and were greeted by Maurice and Barry, tongues lolling as they competed for pets. Five women—all good friends of Lola's—were already in her kitchen heating up casseroles, putting out snacks, and pouring fishbowl-sized glasses of wine. I didn't even know how they'd known to come.

We walked in the door, and Bonnie Hernandez enveloped Lola in a hug. "We got the news alert from the *Free Press*. We let ourselves in with the key you keep behind the ceramic cat on the porch." She pointed.

I cringed. I'd made that for Lola and Kyle in art class. It wasn't a cat. Or at least it wasn't supposed to be a cat. It was supposed to be a horse. Whatever. And as to how they knew, well, apparently all the cool kids had the *Free Press* app and everyone knew where Lola and Kyle hid their extra keys.

Cheryl Cooper, always first on the scene with baked goods, shooed me out the door. "We've got it from here," she said.

I went back to the Element, shook a piece of the gravel from the driveway out of my shoe, and gave Maurice a scratch between the ears. I looked up the hill at Rosemarie and Alan's place. It was hard to believe the situation had come to this. There'd been a time when Rosemarie and Alan had been friends with Lola and Kyle. They'd help each other trim trees and they'd share tools. They'd sit on the deck during the summer sipping wine and watching the sunset, chatting about nothing. Now it was a feud and someone—other than an emu—was dead. Behind me, I could hear the soprano melody of Lola's friends fussing and buzzing around her. It was a stark contrast to the complete lack of sound coming from Rosemarie's house.

No one's car sat in Rosemarie's driveway. No one appeared to be bringing her casseroles or pouring her a glass of wine, although I suppose they all had when it had first happened. I felt a pang of sadness for her. Then I felt a tiny rivulet of sweat slide between my shoulder blades and trickle down my spine. I kicked off my shoes, stripped off my panty hose, got in my car, and drove home barefoot. I needed to get to Tappiano's to meet Jasmine.

Chapter Four

Once I got home, I went upstairs to the room that had been mine since forever but hadn't really been mine for the past decade. I blew out a breath as I walked in, feeling both relief and exasperation. Dad hadn't changed the room since I'd left for college. He hadn't turned it into an office. He hadn't used it for storage. He hadn't taken up weaving and set up a loom. It was exactly as I left it when I'd packed up and gone to UC San Diego.

In the years in between, it had never occurred to me to change anything about it either. The framed Maxfield Parrish poster of the girl sitting on the rock was still on one wall; a poster of a kitten exhorting me to "hang in there" while hanging from a branch was on the opposite wall. The bedspread was still pink gingham, and the desk and dresser were still white. It was sweet and girlish and totally not my style anymore. Why would I have changed it though? I was never here for more than a week at a time, first on school vacations and then on quick trips home with the meager amount of days off I had from the WXYZ Radio news desk and KLVX TV. This room had never been more than a stopping-off point between places I was going once I'd left.

But now . . . now I didn't know how long I'd be here. Now I didn't have a plan. Now I didn't have a place I was going, and the dreamy pastel girl on the rock looking up at the sky no longer spoke to my soul the way it had when I was fifteen. In fact, she pissed me off a little. I took the poster off the wall and shoved it in the closet. Then I flipped off the kitten and pulled it down too. I felt a little better.

I peeled off the rest of my assistant funeral director clothes; changed into a tank top and a short, flowered skirt with sandals; and put on my charm bracelet that jangled a little too happily for the whole "somber funeral" thing. That made me feel a little better too. More me. Less whoever I was pretending to be now.

I stepped out of the air-conditioned chill of Turner Family Funeral Home (seventy-two degrees rain or shine, summer or winter) and back into the full-blast furnace. Even though the peak heat of the day had now passed, it was still probably in the nineties, and the air had the dusty feel of a place that hadn't had rain in months. Because it hadn't. Not since sometime in March. The land stretched away from me, down the long drive lined with crepe myrtle and ornamental plum trees—riots of pink flowers and purple leaves. Miles away, the Vaca Mountains loomed, lavender against the pale blue of the cloudless sky.

I took in a deep breath and inhaled the scents of dust and hay with a tinge of tomatoes from the romas that had fallen from trucks on the way to the processing plants in Williams and were now crushed on the side of the road. In the distance, I could hear the high school band practicing. Home. I took a long swig from my water bottle and stepped off the porch.

I walked past the Cut 'n' Curl; the In-n-Out; the Dollar General; the Count on Me Bookkeepers, which had sprung up after I left home; and the Clean Green Car Wash ("You can keep it clean while staying green!"), which was even newer than all the rest, and finally reached Tappiano's.

Tappiano's was a wine bar before wine bars were trendy. They had had a tasting area when tasting rooms in Napa were still free and nobody went there. They made hand-crafted wines before anyone called anything artisanal and made flavored olive oils before "extra-virgin" was in anyone's lexicon. It was the place to go to get a glass of wine back when the floor was hard-packed dirt and still was now that the floor was bamboo. It was at least partly due to the clever stewardship of Mark Tappiano, great-grandson of the original Tappiano who had started the place.

For instance, I was not the only person to graduate from Verbena High and hit the ground running while the strains of "Pomp and Circumstance" still echoed in the air. A lot of us hightailed it out of town. Verbena High had a pretty decent reputation and a lot of teachers like Lola who knew their subjects and cared about their students. We scattered to dozens of different colleges and universities around California and beyond. None of us thought we'd ever come back. Who would want to?

Turned out that ten years later, a bunch of us had. We were back for lots of different reasons from the quality of the schools and the price of housing to helping out aging parents, but back we were. As far as I knew, I was the only one who came home because she'd humiliated herself on live television and had her gaffe go viral. I've always been special.

Mark Tappiano had seen a marketing opportunity in all of us coming home though. Forget Ladies' Night or Two-fer Tuesdays—he started the Hometown Happy Hour. If you could point to your picture in any one of the dozens of Verbena High yearbooks he kept on the shelves, you got your drinks half price from five to seven.

Judging by the noise level inside Tappiano's when I walked in, happy hour had been going for a while. I stepped inside and paused for a second to let the air conditioning and the noise wash over me. Before I could take another step, I heard someone shout, "Death Ray! You made it! Hey, everyone! Death Ray is here."

There it was again. That nickname. From the first day of kindergarten, I was known as the girl who lived in the mortuary. I hadn't known there was anything weird about it until then. To me, it had been normal. My classmates made sure to enlighten me otherwise. By junior high, I was also the girl with the dead mom. Death hung around me like a cloud. The young and the beautiful have a nearly lizard-brain response to that: avoid it at all costs. They don't even know why. They just do. Then there was the nickname. I blamed Luke Butler, but it probably would have been someone else if it hadn't been him. It hadn't been too hard for elementary school minds to go from Desiree to Deathiree, and from there it was one easy step to Death Ray. Death Ray stuck like glue. Crack open my high school yearbook, and I'd guess that three-quarters of the inscriptions are addressed, "Dear Death Ray." That's what everyone called me.

I pretended that I didn't care, but getting away from being known as Death Ray was one of the reasons I'd left Verbena—and one of the reasons I was not happy to be back.

I gave a halfhearted wave and ducked to the side of the room where I'd spotted Jasmine. Jasmine had been my best friend since I could understand the concept of friendship. We'd gone to the same hippy-dippy preschool, and our mothers had bonded over playdate scheduling, making organic playdough, and stocking the dress-up box with gender-neutral costumes. Jaz and I bonded over one-hundred-percent-natural juice boxes and whole wheat graham crackers. When my mother passed away, Jasmine's mom was another person who stepped in to fill the gap. She's the one who took me to buy my first bra, explained tampons to me, and tucked a Costco-sized package of condoms in my backpack when I left for college. Dad was awesome, but he got a little squeamish when it came to the girl stuff.

Jaz and I might as well have been sisters except for the very noticeable difference in our skin tones. I came in more of a mayonnaise-like tint, while Jaz was more mocha. And our figures. She had the kind of curves that made people stop talking when she walked by. I was . . . sporty. I made it to her table, picked up her wineglass, and sucked down half of something pink.

"Hey," she said. "That's mine."

I nodded toward the crowd. "You expect me to face that without any liquid courage?"

"Ignore them. You always have," she said, raising her hand and waving at the waitress. The waitress, a cute honey-blonde thing, nodded. Jasmine held up two fingers. The waitress nodded again and showed up with a second glass and a bottle of the same pink liquid.

"I thought we didn't drink pink liquor anymore," I said. We'd drunk plenty of pink stuff back in the day. And green. And purple. Somewhere along the way, we'd stopped wanting wine to taste like soda pop though.

"We started again when Tappiano's started making a decent rosé." Jasmine turned to the waitress. "Thanks, Monique. When did you start working here anyway?"

"Like, a couple of weeks ago? I wanted to make some extra cash?" Her sentences all went up at the end as if she were asking us whether or not she wanted to make more money.

"Are you still working at Cold Clutch Canyon Café too?" Jasmine asked.

"I do the morning shift there, then head to my classes at the community college, then back here for happy hour a couple nights a week?" Monique set the glass down and poured us each a healthy serving.

"Busy," I said, impressed. I'd been driven, and I didn't think I'd ever juggled that many things at once.

"I like it that way?" she said. She smiled. She had a dimple. And freckles. She was cute and fresh and had a perky butt and made me feel old. And tired.

Monique left and Jasmine turned back to me. "How's Lola holding up?"

"Not that great. It's like she's sleepwalking." I turned to look out the window and watched a dirty pickup truck pull into the Clean Green Car Wash. A man got out of the truck and handed his keys to a car-wash attendant. He was the kind of guy you noticed. He looked a little like a turtle with a head cold, and he was wearing what looked like a kurta pajama set. The attendant pulled the truck around toward the back of the car wash. "It's all ridiculous, though. I can't believe Luke could even imagine that Kyle would kill someone. Who would get that angry over a neighborhood dispute anyway?"

Jasmine turned to face the window too and gazed out at the car wash. "There's a lot more anger in this town than you realize. Stuff simmers for long enough, and then it just blows up. People want to get in the last word and escalate situations until they turn violent. People get obsessed about something and chase after it in ways that aren't healthy."

"In Verbena?" That didn't seem right, but if anybody would know, it was Jasmine. She'd established her therapy practice here right after she'd been licensed and hadn't had a free day since. She'd shrunk half the town in the past three years.

The car-wash attendant brought the truck back and handed the man the keys. He got into his truck and drove away. I was surprised he hadn't complained. It didn't look like they'd washed his truck at all. Mud still spattered the wheel wells, and dirt streaked down the sides.

"Totally in Verbena. I run a regular Saturday anger management session, and there are always plenty of people there. Every week." She looked down at the table and turned her wineglass in circles. "Plenty," she reiterated.

That gave me something to think about. Angers simmered. People got violent. Not Kyle, though. Never Kyle. But someone. Someone had gotten angry enough to kill. Somewhere underneath Verbena's placid small-town exterior, roiling emotions worked. I'd been away too long. I didn't know all the little feuds and skirmishes that simmered. Jasmine, however, had been right here and had a front-row seat into a lot of the town's true fears and obsessions. "So who hates Alan Brewer?"

"Besides Kyle and Lola?" Jasmine asked. She twirled her stool around to face me.

I shot her a look. "Yes, besides Kyle and Lola."

"He's a banker, Desiree. Everybody hates bankers these days." Jasmine finished her wine, pulled some cash out of her wallet, and put it on the table. "Give you a ride home?"

"Thanks." I plunked some money down too. Walking had seemed a good idea before I'd had wine on a nearly empty stomach. Now the idea of weaving home in the heat was significantly less appealing.

We left Tappiano's, pausing as we stepped out onto the sidewalk to adjust to the twenty-degree swing in temperature from inside to out, and walked over to where Jasmine's Subaru was parked near her office. "What's that on your hood?" I asked, squinting, when we were about half a block away. There was a small box on the hood of her car, and it looked like whatever was inside had leaked out.

Jasmine's steps slowed. "I'm not sure."

We approached the car as if it were some kind of animal that might suddenly lunge at us. Whatever had leaked out of the box was brown and puddling on the hood. "Is that . . . ?" I didn't even want to finish the thought.

Jasmine straightened, took two more steps forward, jammed her finger into the brown puddle, and stuck her finger in her mouth.

I screamed.

"Chocolate," she said. "Want a taste?"

"Oh." I stepped closer and could smell the chocolate now. I could also see the box. See's Candy. A local delicacy, but not outside on a hot summer day. "Who would leave chocolate out on a one-hundred-degree day?" I asked.

She looked around with narrowed eyes. "Someone new. Someone who wouldn't realize what our heat does to chocolate."

We wiped the chocolate off the car as best we could with the wet wipes Jaz kept in her car. Then we got in, licking our fingers and laughing. As we pulled out of the parking space and into the street, I thought for a second I saw someone coming out of the doorway of one of the shops. I started to say something, then I saw a squad car pulling into the street in the opposite direction that we were driving. I thought the driver was that female officer that had been at the desk when Kyle was arrested. I settled back in my seat. If there was anything or anyone there, she'd deal with it.

Chapter Five

I slipped in the back entrance once I got home. Our living quarters took up the third floor with back stairs that let us go in and out without going into the funeral parlor itself. I could hear the television in the family room and poked my head in. Uncle Joey sat in the big recliner chair that he filled completely and then some. Donna was on the couch, long legs extended and her feet in the lap of her husband, Greg. Her blonde hair gleamed in the lamplight while she crocheted something pink. Greg rubbed her feet. It all looked so peaceful until Donna turned around and saw me and I could see the fire in her eyes. "Where have you been?"

I gulped. It hadn't occurred to me to tell anyone where I was going or why. In my decade away, I'd become pretty accustomed to not reporting to anyone when I came or went. "Kyle Hansen was arrested. I went to the jail to help Lola out and then . . ."

Donna sniffed the air. "Then you went for drinks with Jasmine?"

I felt the heat creep up my face.

Donna said, "Can I talk to you?"

I sighed. "Sure." I trooped to the kitchen, ready to take whatever was coming my way.

Donna walked in after me. "You steamed out of here without letting anyone know and with people still in the Lilac Room." She winced.

"I'm sorry. I got so caught up in Kyle drama, I didn't think." I hadn't either. Not a jot. My stomach twisted.

"This on top of the disaster at Miss Delia's funeral. You said you could handle it." She glared at me. Donna was two years older than me. We couldn't be more different. It wasn't just our looks. She'd wanted to stay in Verbena and work in the family business. I couldn't wait to be away from it. She wanted to settle down and have kids. I was pretty sure I was still a kid myself. That didn't mean I didn't want her respect, though. There was nothing for it. I had said I'd handle Miss Delia's service, and I hadn't. Or at least not well. "I thought I could."

Donna sat down across the table from me with a small thump. "Miss Delia's service should have been the biggest no-brainer of the week. She had everything mapped out. *Everything.* Music. Seating. Food. Timing."

"I know." I sunk down in my chair a little bit.

44

Donna made a face, and her hand dropped to her tummy, bringing me back to the moment. "I can't do this by myself right now, Desiree. I need your help," she said.

I knew that too. Since she found out she was pregnant, Donna had been on light duty. Some of the chemicals downstairs could be nasty, and it seemed smart to stay away from them. Uncle Joey could take care of all that, no problem. He hadn't ever had to handle the front office stuff, though. That had been Dad's role. Donna had been learning both sides of the trade, but she needed a break now. She'd lost one pregnancy already. It wasn't that uncommon. Miscarriages happen more frequently than most people know. But the timing had been awful. She'd lost the baby weeks after Dad disappeared. It had been a crushing blow on top of a horrible loss.

Sixteen months ago, our father had gone surfing and hadn't come back. Dad surfed alone all the time. It wasn't unusual for him to get up at the butt-crack of dawn, drive to Salmon Creek, surf for a couple of hours, and be back in time for an afternoon memorial service.

Back when I lived at home, I'd go with him sometimes. No one else in the family shared his passion for floating out on the ocean, waiting for a big curl to ride into shore. Donna said it was terrifying, and the last time Dad had talked her into going with him, she'd had nightmares about drowning for two weeks afterward. Uncle Joey said that if he was going to be on the water, he'd like

45

to be in a boat, thank you very much. Both of them now ardently wished they'd been a little more flexible.

With me gone, Dad went alone. He'd pack up his board and his wetsuit and go. The last time he did, he didn't make the return trip. Thinking about it now made me feel like I was drowning.

The first I'd known about anything being wrong was a phone call from Uncle Joey. Had I heard from Dad? Had he called? Texted? E-mailed? Left a message? Anything in the last twenty-four hours? Anything at all?

He hadn't. No one had heard anything. I'd been on the next plane home, but even that takes time. That's why it was close to forty-eight hours from the last time anyone had heard from him or seen him—he'd had dinner with Donna and Greg the night before—to when I found his Honda Element parked on the verge by Salmon Creek. His phone and wallet and a stack of dry clothes to put on postsurf were all there. Everything was there except Dad.

None of it was important, except Dad.

The next month was spent searching shorelines, checking hospitals, looking at every John Doe along California's northern coastline, dead or alive. We never found him. Not a trace. Not even his board.

He'd been so pleased about his first grandchild. To have that ripped away along with him had made it all that much more devastating. None of us had fared well.

Donna had spent days in her room, eyes swollen from crying. Uncle Joey had moved through his days like a big Viking version of a robot. I'd gone back to Los Angeles thinking I could jump right back into my job with no problem and instead I torpedoed my career. It had been more than a year and we were all just finding our footing again. We were all coming out of our self-imposed bubbles of misery and leaning on each other to get better. It was the one good thing about me coming home. I could help my family.

With me home, Donna could spend most of her time off her feet in the back office dealing with the mountains of paperwork that death required, Uncle Joey could handle all the work in the basement, and I could take over the front office stuff that Dad had always handled. The hole Dad's disappearance had left in our lives and our hearts would never be filled, but it didn't have to be an open wound.

Except I'd pretty much failed at the handling on my first solo flight. "I'll do better," I promised. I'd let so many people down already, I couldn't stand the idea of letting down Donna when she needed me. It wasn't entirely my fault, though. It wasn't like I'd mixed up the music or forgotten to put out the programs. "I swear no one could have stopped that. Not even Dad."

She sighed. "If you say so." She winced and put her hand on her tummy.

"Are you okay?" I asked. "Why don't you go back to the couch? There's really nothing for me to screw up at the moment."

"Well, don't go looking for anything." She frowned at me and left.

I put my head down on the old oak table. I didn't need to look for things to screw up. They seemed to find me all by themselves.

Chapter Six

The Verbena Free Press

MONDAY, JULY 15

Arrest Made in Local Murder

Kyle Hansen, longtime resident of Verbena, has been arrested for the murder of Alan Brewer. Hansen and Brewer were neighbors and had become involved in a dispute that began with the death of the Brewers' beloved pet emu and escalated into a civil suit. Brewer's wife, Rosemarie, and Hansen's wife, Lola, had been involved in an altercation during the funeral of beloved local Delia Burns.

Pursuant to that altercation, Ms. Hansen had received notice that her job teaching at Verbena High could be in jeopardy due to her violating the morals clause in her contract.

According to Hansen's lawyer, Janet Provost, Hansen plans to plead not guilty. "We'll plead not guilty because Kyle isn't guilty. It's that simple," said Provost. Prosecuting Attorney Tommy Lomax responded with the following statement: "There is a preponderance of evidence stacked up against Mr. Hansen. We will present all that evidence in court and have no doubt that Mr. Hansen will be found guilty by a jury of his peers."

Ms. Brewer said, "I shouldn't be surprised. The Hansens and their vicious attack dogs have shown no respect for other beings' lives. We tried to tell people after the death of Vincent, but no one listened. Now here we are with my husband dead at the hands of that monster."

Hansen's arraignment is set for next week. For details on services for Alan Brewer, contact Desiree Turner at Turner Family Funeral Home.

The next morning, I rolled out of bed a little after five AM. If you want to spend any time outdoors in Verbena in the summertime, you'd best do it early. Since I had a twenty-minute drive to where I wanted to be outside, it needed to be extra early. Apparently, not earlier than little Sam Wasnowski—he had already delivered the *Verbena Free Press* to our front door. I checked the front page and found myself above the fold again.

I slid the page with the article about Kyle out of its section and shoved it in the recycling. With any luck, Donna wouldn't even notice it was missing. If she didn't see it, maybe she wouldn't get mad at me. How the heck did my name keep getting in those articles, anyway? How did a consistent string of "no comments" merit that much ink?

I brushed my teeth; laced up my hiking boots; grabbed water, a granola bar, and an apple; and was out the door by five thirty. The sun was rising as I drove to the Cold Clutch Canyon Trailhead, starting as a yellow glow on the horizon and spreading across the flat farmland between Verbena and the Vaca Mountains. Then the light went orange and pink with a little purple around the edge. The mountains shimmered against the sky. There was a moment when it all changed, when dark became light and the sky went blue. It was sort of like the green flash you sometimes get to see at sunset on the beach, but in reverse. I plugged my dad's old Beatles CD into the player and listened to George Harrison tell me that the sun was coming. I drove past a field of sunflowers, heads all bent in the same direction, ready to track the sun across the cloudless California sky.

By the time I made it to the trailhead, the sun was completely up, but the air was still cool and fresh. I was the third car in the parking lot. I recognized Carol Burston's Prius. She actually ran the four-mile loop I was about to walk. She did it at least three times a week. I had never been that ambitious, but I got out here at least once a week or so and hiked it. The other car was an Element like mine. A little newer and gray instead of black. I was jealous. Sometimes Dad's Element would get so hot I couldn't touch it. Black totally absorbs heat, but Dad

51

always insisted on driving a black vehicle. Sometimes the funeral business could be unforgiving.

I started off on the first leg of the trail, which would take me up about fifteen hundred feet. By halfway, I was panting from the change in altitude. I pushed through it as I went past the manzanita bushes and bunchgrasses, breathing in the sharp green scent of sage. There were still black patches here and there from the King Snake Fire a few years before. I'd cried when I'd seen the news reports that had showed the hills I'd loved so much burning. It had raged for days before they got it under control. I'd been in Los Angeles and probably hadn't hiked Cold Clutch for a couple of years at that point, but it still hurt to see my beloved hills engulfed in flames. Nature was resilient, though. All around, green shoots came up through the blackened soil. Rebirth. I felt my chest open a bit, and suddenly it seemed easier to breathe.

Dad and I used to do this hike. It was one of our things, along with surfing. Trudging up the incline. Scrambling over the rocks. We'd never talked much, not like Donna and Dad had. But we'd climb this grade together, find a place on the ridge with a view over the lake, eat our breakfast, and climb back down. I don't remember how old I was the first time we did it. I remember it was after Mom died, so I had to be at least nine.

A Swainson's hawk soared over me, and my mood soared with it. I had one ledge in particular that I liked to sit on. By some geological wonder, there was a depression in it that matched my butt almost exactly. I sat, drank my water, ate my apple, breathed in the air, and felt the early morning sunshine beginning to warm the day.

I tossed my apple core into the brush for some enterprising bunny or squirrel, then I headed back down the other side. It wasn't as steep, but it was a lot more rocky. I had no idea how Carol ran it without twisting an ankle. It was worth it, though, to go past the outline of the old cabin that used to stand halfway down. It was one of the last places I played make-believe. Somehow it had still been okay to be a little girl there with only my dad watching. Somehow there had still been a little magic in the world early in the morning as the sun broke through the trees, dappling the rocks and old timber with weak light. Somehow I had been safe there.

Today, when I stopped to play make-believe, I wasn't pretending I was Snow White waiting for the dwarves to come home or Laura Ingalls Wilder in the Big Woods. I pretended that my dad was still there, and for a second or two, it felt like he was. I felt the warmth of his gaze on me, the safety I'd always felt when he was around, the knowledge of unconditional love. Then behind me I heard someone coming and started down the path again.

I got back to the car and finished my water, leaning against the side of the car. If I hadn't done that, I'm not sure I would have spotted it. It was just a little glint in the sun as I made designs with the toe of my hiking boot in the gravel of the parking lot. Just a tiny bit of sparkle on the floorboard.

I crouched down and brushed the dirt away. It was a tiny silver hiking boot with an eye-ring on top—a charm. Just like the charms on my own charm bracelet. The ones my dad bought me for every occasion. Birthdays. Holidays. Graduations. I had two bracelets full of them. This could easily have been one of them that had maybe fallen off in the car when I'd worn the bracelet and then gotten kicked out into the parking lot when I'd exited.

Except I didn't have a charm of a hiking boot. Dad hadn't bought me one of those. Or if he had, he hadn't given it to me yet when he disappeared. I looked around the parking lot to see if there was anyone it could belong to, but I was alone. The other cars were gone. I slipped the charm into my pocket and got in the car.

*   *   *

Janet Provost and Lola were waiting for me in the lobby of the police station. Janet looked exactly as she had on the volleyball sidelines ten years before. She had on a pair of capri pants and a multicolored top and a pair of flip-flops with some bling on them. Her dark hair was sensibly cut into one of those mom cuts, kind of a cross between Kris Jenner and Kate Gosselin. I gave her a hug.

"Desiree, honey, how are you?" Janet took me by the shoulders and held me out at arm's length. She smelled like roses. "You look wonderful. Are you wonderful?"

I looked down at the sundress I was wearing and tried to figure out whether or not it was wonderful. "Working on it," I said, not sure how else to respond.

"Aren't we all always a work in progress?" She tucked me against her side. I sunk in as if she was upholstery. She pointed to a covered plate sitting on the chair next to Lola. "Muffins?" she asked.

I shook my head. "Already had breakfast."

"That wouldn't stop me—unfortunately," she said as she patted her stomach. "But let's go ahead in."

I gave Lola a hug as she stood up. It felt as if she'd shrunk a little more already. "Are you okay?"

She shook her head. "No, but I can fake it."

"We're here to see Kyle Hansen," I told the officer at the front desk, who didn't really look old enough to be holding any kind of weapon more lethal than a squirt gun.

"You on his list?" he asked, not looking up from the form in front of him.

"Yes. I'm his lawyer, and I made sure all our names were on the list." Janet bristled up like she was ready for a fight. None came.

"ID, please." He stuck out his hand, still not looking at us.

I dug my driver's license out of my wallet and put it in his outstretched hand. Lola and Janet did the same.

He looked at the licenses, made a note on a pad, handed them back to us, and indicated the door behind me with a head nod.

"Empty your pockets, and put your purse in here." He shoved a bin in front of me.

I looked down at the sundress I was wearing. What pockets did he think I had to empty? I dropped my purse in the bin.

"What about this?" Janet held up the plate of muffins.

"What is it?" he asked.

She pulled back the foil cover to show him.

"I don't think you can take that in there," he said, looking uneasy.

"It's not like there's a file in it," Janet said and laughed.

He looked even more uneasy, like maybe she wasn't joking about a file. "Afraid not," he said, shaking his head.

"Too bad. Have some yourself then," Janet said, shoving the plate at him. "Don't make me take that home, young man!" She waggled a finger at him.

We ended up in a room with a fluorescent overhead light, a metal table, and hard plastic chairs. I glanced around for the two-way mirror you see in all the cop shows. Instead I spotted a small video camera in the corner. "Will anyone be listening to us?"

"No, ma'am. Knock on the door if there's trouble and you need me to come. Otherwise, I'll be back in fifteen minutes."

A few minutes later, another officer ushered in Kyle. He looked like he'd aged about ten years. "Lola," he said, a wealth of meaning in the name.

"Kyle." She stepped toward him as he opened his arms as far as the chain would allow.

The officer raised his hand. "No touching, please." He proceeded to lock Kyle's handcuffs to a metal ring in the center of the table. So I wouldn't get one of those hugs that reminded me so much of my dad. I hadn't realized how much I'd been counting on that.

I cringed as the cuffs clicked closed. "You don't have to do that. He's not going to hurt us."

"It's procedure" was the only reply. Then the officer left.

We all sat back. "Are you okay?" I asked.

Kyle shook his head. "I suppose as okay as can be expected. This is insane, Desiree. I would never kill a person. I would certainly never kill a person over . . . over nothing."

"I know that, Kyle. Anyone with half a brain in his head would know that. Unfortunately, that doesn't seem to include Luke Butler." Despite the gun and the neighborhood squabbles and everything else, I still thought Luke should have known better.

"Maybe we can construct a timeline that would show you couldn't have done it. Nate has set the time of death for approximately six forty-five," Janet said, glancing at her notes. "Tell me about that morning. Where were you? What did you do?"

"I did the same thing I do every morning. I got up, had a cup of coffee, pulled on some clothes, and took Maurice and Barry for a walk." He looked over at Lola as if for confirmation. She nodded.

"What time?" I asked.

He blew out a breath. "Alarm goes off at six. I'm usually out the door by six thirty. We walk for about an hour—however long it takes me to get up the road to Mobley's place on the hill—then we turn around and come home."

"Same route every day?" I asked.

"Except sometimes when Lola comes with us. She likes to walk down by the creek. I don't like having to clean the mud off the dog's paws every day, so I don't usually go that way."

"Same time every day?" I asked.

"Pretty much. Not if it's raining or too windy. Then we stay home," he said.

We weren't likely to have too much rain or wind this time of year. This was so Kyle: dependable, predictable. Had those two things that I prized in him actually gotten him into this mess? Doing the same things at the same times each day would make him easy to frame for something he didn't do.

"Did you see anyone?" I asked. It would help if someone could confirm what he was saying.

He shook his head. "No, no one. It's pretty quiet out there at that time of day. It's part of why I like to walk then."

"Who knows that's your routine?" Janet asked.

He tried to throw his hands in the air, but he couldn't because of the chains. He winced as he pulled against them. "How would I know that? I suppose if you watched, you'd figure out pretty quickly, but who pays attention to stuff like that?"

I hated to tell him that lots of people pay attention to things like that. People are nosy. People are curious. "Do you lock the house when you leave?"

He shook his head. "Not usually. Nobody really comes out that way."

"And you still keep a key outside?" I asked. They always had when I was a kid.

"Sure. It's in that ceramic frog you made for me and Lola in art class." He smiled.

I blushed. It wasn't a frog. It was a horse. Art was never my thing. "How many people know that?"

Kyle rested his head on his folded hands. "How should I know that? Honestly, I don't spend a lot of my life looking around to see who's watching me."

It was one of the things my dad had loved about Kyle. He really didn't care who was watching. He led his life so that he could be an open book, just like Dad had. There was a reason they were best friends. "Did you hear anything when you were out on your walk? Did you hear the gunshot?"

"The police have asked me that over and over. I wish I could remember, but you know what it's like out there. It's not that uncommon of a sound. It's not like in town, where you would register that noise and think about it." He leaned down so he could rub his forehead.

"So you don't remember hearing it?" Janet asked, making some notes.

He sighed. "No, I don't."

"Do you remember hearing anything else? Seeing anything else?" I asked.

"Saw a deer." He smiled.

Again, so Kyle. "I mean anything that might pertain to Alan's murder," Janet said.

He shook his head. "Sorry, no."

"We should go, then. If you think of anything, make sure to tell one of us. Don't tell anybody else, though. Nobody else here in the cells with you. None of the cops," she warned.

He shook his head. "Oh, come on, Janet. I've known most of these kids in here since they were in Lola's classes at the high school. None of them is in for anything more serious than drunk and disorderly or vandalism."

"I know that. That's why I'm warning you. They're not on your side this time."

She was right. I'd seen too many people get ratted out by someone making a side deal. "Anything you tell them, they can tell someone else, and someone else can twist those words to benefit their side."

He sighed. "I wish there weren't sides to take."

That was again so Kyle. I risked breaking the no-touching rule to put my hand over his. "We'll get this straightened out."

He put his free hand over mine and gave a rueful laugh. "You sound just like your dad."

Gosh darn it. I swore something got in my eye right then.

Chapter Seven

I screwed up my courage, called Nate, and convinced him to meet me for a cup of coffee at the Cold Clutch Canyon Café.

I slipped into a booth there and Monique, the same perky honey-blonde waitress that had brought me my rosé the night before, poured me a cup of coffee in one of those thick china mugs that you seem to only find at diners. A few minutes later, Nate slid into the booth across from me.

"Hi, Desiree."

Nate had never called me Death Ray. Not once. Nate Johar didn't care that there were dead people in my basement or that my mom was dead. Nate Johar cared that I made him laugh. He cared that I liked action movies. And on at least one memorable night before we both left for college, he cared that I didn't always wear a bra.

That night was a long time ago, though. Now he ran his hands through his hair. It looked nicely rumpled, like he'd just got out of bed. Monique poured him a cup of coffee.

"So you're back here for good?" he asked, adding cream and taking a sip.

"I don't know." I looked down at the table. "I'm still trying to figure that out."

"It's a nice place, you know." He wrapped his hands around the mug. His fingers were incredibly long, like practically E.T. long.

Verbena was nice. It was also small. And gossipy. And full of obligations. "I'm pretty aware of what it's like here." I sighed. "How are your parents?"

He shrugged. "Good. Dad made vice president at NatureTech and plays a lot of golf. Mom took up quilting."

"That's nice." His parents had never been thrilled about me. It was nothing personal. They would have preferred for Nate to date a nice Indian girl or possibly not to date at all and focus on studying.

He took another sip of coffee. "It's good to see you again. Even better when it's not over a dead body."

"About that: I don't suppose you found anything interesting when you did the autopsy?" I asked, trying to keep my voice neutral.

His eyes narrowed. "What do you mean by interesting?"

I shrugged, going for nonchalance. "I don't know. Something that might indicate who had actually done it?"

"You mean like something out of a television show where they can determine the exact height of the shooter based on bullet trajectory?" he asked. "Or the presence of a certain kind of dust on the victim's shoes that would point to the killer?"

I sat up straighter. Terrific! Nate had found something that would exonerate Kyle. "Yes, exactly like that. That would be really helpful."

He leaned toward me. "No, there was nothing like that. Alan died from the bullet wound to his forehead by his own chicken coop on his own land."

I slumped down again. "Anything in his stomach contents or something that might point to a particular person?" I asked.

He shook his head. "I don't believe this. You get me down here on the pretense of wanting to catch up when all you want to do is pick my brains about Alan Brewer's autopsy?"

I blushed. The bait and switch had been entirely intentional. I had a good reason, though. "Kyle didn't do it, Nate. I need to find a way to prove it."

"Since when did solving murders fall under the purview of assistant funeral directors?" he asked.

"It doesn't, but when the local police have arrested the wrong person and refuse to investigate any further, someone has to do something." I started to feel indignant.

"I know how you feel about Kyle, Desiree. I know how close he was to your father. Luke wouldn't have made the arrest lightly, though. If he felt he had enough evidence for an arrest, he probably has a pretty sound case."

I signaled to Monique to refill my mug. "It's all circumstantial. Kyle did not kill Alan." I leapt back as Monique overfilled my mug and coffee spilled across the table.

"Sorry!" she gasped. "Sorry." She grabbed a towel that had been stuck in the waistband of her apron and mopped up the coffee. She looked like she might cry. The girl must really need the tips.

"It's okay," I said, patting her hand. No one should feel that bad over a spilled cup of coffee.

"Yes," said Nate. "We were done anyway."

After she walked away, I asked, "We were done?"

"Yes, we were done. I have nothing to tell you except that the postmortem is done and I'm releasing his body for burial. There was nothing in the autopsy that pointed to anyone in particular, and if there was, I'm not sure I'd tell you. It's not your job." He folded his arms over his chest. "This is because Luke Butler is the one who arrested Kyle, isn't it?"

"No." I picked at a seam on the seat of the upholstered booth.

"Desiree, this is not a student council election. This is a murder investigation. There's no room in it for petty childhood squabbles." He stood. "I'm leaving now."

I sat at the booth, finishing my coffee and thinking about what Nate had just said. What I was doing *was* about Kyle. I was sure of that. I wasn't sure that the idea of showing Luke Butler he was wrong about something didn't add a little bit of luster to the project. We'd been rivals throughout high school. Always competing for the same spots, jockeying for position. The worst was the campaign for senior class president. I'd run a carefully thought-through campaign focused on getting more organic food into the cafeteria and lengthening library hours. Luke had whipped everyone up into a frenzy with cheers and chants and had beaten me. I still didn't understand it. It had been my first and last dalliance with politics beyond covering local elections.

My reverie was interrupted by my cell phone ringing. I looked at the caller ID. It was Donna. "What's up, buttercup?"

"Desiree, I'm bleeding."

* * *

A Grave Issue

Waiting rooms are such weird interstitial spaces. Everyone there is in some kind of limbo, in between one state and the next. The one at Verbena Memorial was actually nicer than most. I'd been in some down in Los Angeles covering car accidents and fires that were downright nasty. Plastic molded chairs. Dirty cracked linoleum floors. Corners full of the kind of weird dust and debris that made you worry about tetanus and hepatitis. Harsh fluorescent lights, always with one blinking on and off at random intervals. People huddled, holding blood-soaked rags to injuries.

The lighting in this one was soft, and the magazines were no more than three months old. The chairs were cushioned. The floor was carpeted. I could see vacuum marks on the carpet, and it smelled like lemon wood polish. It was practically a luxury suite.

I didn't care.

I'd been prowling from wall to wall for twenty-five minutes when Greg showed up.

"Where is she?" he asked, looking wild-eyed.

It wasn't his normal look. His normal look was placid, calm, unruffled, handsome in that kind of bland way of symmetrical features and hair that seemed to fall the right way. Of course, the situation wasn't normal. There was something wrong with Donna or the baby. Not normal at all.

"I'm not totally sure where she is. They took her back to a room and shuffled me into here once they decided to admit her. The nurse at the desk said they'd come get me when I could go in." It was all I knew, and it was clearly cold comfort.

He sank into one of the chairs. "What happened?"

"I don't know. She wasn't feeling well, so she stayed in bed, but then she called me . . ." And I'd run back home and taken the stairs two at a time to get back to her. I barely remembered the drive to the hospital.

He rubbed his hands across his face. "I knew something wasn't right. She won't tell me when she doesn't feel good. She doesn't want to worry me. I should have listened to my gut. I should have stayed home."

Before I could comment, Dr. Chao came into the waiting room. She was a short woman with black hair pulled back into a messy ponytail. Her steel-frame glasses were slightly askew as if she'd fallen asleep on them. Her eyes looked puffy. She sat down on the coffee table across from Greg. "First of all, she's fine and the baby is fine."

He blew out a breath and collapsed back in the chair. "Thank goodness."

"For now," she continued.

Next to me, Greg stiffened. "What does that mean?"

"That means we need to be cautious." She put her hand on Greg's knee. "I'd rather err on the side of caution than take unnecessary chances. I think we should put Donna on limited bed rest for a while." She turned to me. "You're the sister?"

"Yep, that's me." The sister. It was like a title.

"So you can take over for her at work, right?" she asked.

"Absolutely." There wasn't anything I could think of that would be more important.

She turned back to Greg. "And, Greg, you can be around more?"

He nodded. "I can take some time off work, stay home with her."

"With her sister and uncle around, I don't think that it will be necessary yet." Dr. Chao shut her eyes for a second.

I didn't like the sound of *yet*. "So this could get worse?"

"That's what we're trying to avoid. Do you want to go back to see her now?" she asked.

Both Greg and I nodded like bobblehead dolls.

There's something about hospital beds that make people look small. I'm not sure why. It's not like those miserable things are huge, yet everyone looks tiny and frail once they're in one. Donna was no exception. A number of machines beeped and booped around her bed. I knew most of them. Blood pressure. Oxygenation. Heart rate. There was another one measuring the baby's heart rate.

I swallowed hard. It never failed to take me back to visiting my mother in the hospital. I knew if I was the one hooked up to the machines, my pulse would be racing and my blood pressure would be spiking up. I didn't have full-blown panic attacks in hospitals anymore. That was years behind me. It didn't mean I liked being there, though. I didn't know if Donna had the same associations or not. Did being here make her scared that she might not be around to raise the little munchkin inside her? Did she worry about our genes? Or some weird fate?

"I'm sorry," Donna said as Greg slid into the chair by her bed. "I didn't want to make a fuss. I didn't want to be a bother."

He took her hand and pressed it to his lips. "Never a bother, and I want to fuss over you all the time forever."

She lowered her eyelashes. "You don't mean that."

"I do," he said. A tear leaked out of the corner of Greg's eye. He brushed it away, looking at his hand as if he was as surprised it was there as anyone else.

Donna's eyes glistened too.

I backed out of the room. Nobody needed their kid sister around at a moment like that. I walked back out of the hospital to where I'd parked the Element after dropping Donna at the emergency department door. The parking lot surface felt soft and sticky beneath my feet. I stepped up my pace, eager to get inside the car and start the air conditioning.

A Grave Issue

I got back to the house and went up to my room, falling on the bed with arms outstretched like I was going to make a snow angel. I stared up at the ceiling and then at the now blank walls. I pulled myself into a sitting position and looked around. The bare walls and the white furniture were like a clean slate. I didn't have to leave it like this. I could make it my own. I could start over.

I grabbed my laptop, and after consulting a few design websites, I decided on what I wanted. I then spent more money than I probably should have on new drapes, new sheets, and a new comforter for the bed. No more pink and gingham for me.

Chapter Eight

With Donna on bed rest, there was no choice but to have me deal with Rosemarie when she came in to make the arrangements for Alan's funeral. I'd been a little surprised that she wanted to have us as her funeral home. I'd thought she might have bad feelings about us after the whole Miss Delia debacle, but we're pretty much the only funeral game in town, and that hadn't really been our fault.

When she walked in, I saw what Luke meant about her looking like a zombie. Her eyes were red-rimmed and puffy. Her hair hung limply around her face. Her hands shook a tiny bit. I may not have liked the position she'd put Kyle and Lola in, but I couldn't help but have some sympathy for what she was going through. The fact that she was going through it alone made it worse.

Sudden death took its toll. Sheena had been exhausted after years of taking care of her father. She'd been wrung out. She'd been ridden hard and put away wet. She'd also been prepared. She'd known what was coming and even how it was likely to come. She was sad but not shocked. Rosemarie hadn't have time to prepare. The double whammy of shock and grief looked like it was knocking her off her feet.

"How are you doing?" I asked after getting her a glass of water.

"Oh," she said, waving her hand limply in the air. "Okay, I guess. Or as okay as I can be. Can we get this over with?"

It wasn't an uncommon question. A lot of people wanted to get through these decisions as quickly as possible, but there were so many options to choose from. I showed her the various packages we offered to make it easier.

"I'd like to have the viewing here right before the burial," she said, looking at her calendar.

I hesitated. "Do you want an open casket?" That bullet hole in his skull was going to be hard for even an artist like Uncle Joey to work around. "Maybe a visitation would be a better choice."

Her hand went to her mouth and shook a bit. Then she said, "No, I want a viewing. I understand what you're saying. I saw what that evil man did to my Alan. Everyone else should see too. We have nothing to be ashamed about. It's them. They should be ashamed."

I bit my tongue even harder trying not to immediately come to Kyle's defense. I had to compartmentalize. "Friend of Kyle and Lola" Desiree had to stay separate from "assistant funeral director" Desiree. I needed to erect the equivalent of the kind of Chinese wall law firms use to prevent conflicts of interest. "Of course, it's up to you, but maybe you'll want to think a little about that before you make a final decision. We can schedule the time, and you can decide whether to have an open or closed casket later."

She nodded. "Okay. Thank you."

"Did you bring some clothes for him?" I asked.

She picked up the bag she'd been carrying and shoved it at me. I peeked inside and pulled some of the items out.

"He loved that suit. It was his favorite. He always wore it with that shirt and that tie." She pointed to the items.

I looked a little deeper and saw shoes. I folded the items carefully and put them back in the bag. I'd have the suit dry-cleaned and the shirt laundered before we put them on Alan. We covered music and food choices. Next we moved on to the funeral itself.

"Does Alan already have a plot at Lawn of Heaven?" I asked.

Rosemarie shook her head.

"I'll give you the number to call to set up an appointment with the staff there. They can show you your options." The next step was difficult. "Would you like to choose a casket now?"

She nodded again. I ushered her to the second floor, where the showroom was. There are a lot of different kinds of caskets: plain, fancy, extrafancy, caskets with special memory drawers, cloth-covered caskets, steel caskets, solid wood caskets, half couch, full couch, different kinds of linings, and ornaments and additions galore. We also have a whole collection of green eco-friendly caskets now. It's overwhelming, and I hadn't even started describing the urns, which included a line of fine-art urns made by local artists (one of Donna's brainstorms).

"Did you have something in mind already?" I asked.

"Something simple. Something elegant. Something like . . . Alan." Then the tears began to fall, and somehow I was standing in the middle of the casket showroom—where Jasmine and I used to play hide-and-seek—holding Rosemarie Brewer as she sobbed on my shoulder.

No, it wasn't awkward at all.

After I got her calmed down and her selections were made, I tucked the paperwork into the file folder Uncle Joey had made for Alan. Now was the part where we had to talk about money. I took a moment to figure out what everything Rosemarie had chosen would cost. I made sure to give her a set of state-mandated papers that detailed what could and could not be charged and handed it all to her.

She took a moment to go over it all, nodding. Then she pulled an envelope out of her purse and counted out a stack of bills. "This should cover it," she said.

I stared at the pile of cash. It wasn't the way this usually went. "Are you sure you want to pay with cash, Rosemarie?"

She shrugged. "It was in the safe by our wills and passports and birth certificates." Her voice caught on that last item. I guessed what she was thinking—that she'd be filing Alan's death certificate in the same place soon. I reached out to touch her hand, but she pulled it back. "I guess Alan left it there for a moment like this. He was always a planner."

I picked up the stack of money. A strange, damp scent came off of it. It reminded me of when Lola showed me how to dig up bulbs in the garden and separate them. Her daffodils were famous. It wasn't an unpleasant memory, but I generally didn't like to smell that when I opened my wallet. My guess was that the cash would spend fine no matter what it smelled like, though. I'd be depositing it in the bank, anyway. Maybe they could figure out a way to fumigate it.

I walked Rosemarie to the door. Her feet dragged as if she was reluctant to leave and go back home. I didn't blame her. It had been so strange to come back to this house with Dad gone. I expected him to come around the corner any minute, and when he didn't, a fresh wave of grief would wash over me. Donna and I had clung to each other. We'd been each other's solace. Rosemarie was so very alone. Walking back into the house she had shared with Alan must have been especially devastating with no one else there. "Rosemarie, do you have anyone coming to be with you?"

"Why?" She looked confused.

"To help you. This is a rough time. Do you have a friend you could call? A relative?" I asked.

"That's a good idea." She looked around as if someone might materialize.

"Would you like me to call someone for you?" I asked.

Her eyes came back into focus. "No, that won't be necessary. I'm fine."

We walked the rest of the way to the door. She paused before leaving. "Your dad . . . passed unexpectedly, right?"

I leaned against the archway, not sure where this was going. "Yes."

"What did you do about all his passwords and stuff? I don't know how to get into Alan's phone or his computer or his iPad." She made a gesture of helplessness. "He had all our records."

"Well, enough of Dad's stuff was business related that Uncle Joey had most of the passwords." Dad's life had been an open book. It was shared with all of us. Apparently, Alan's wasn't.

"Oh." She looked down for a second. "You said *most*. Not all?"

I thought about that. His laptop had had a password that no one had known. "No, not all. Not his computer."

"What did you do about that?" she asked, more life in her eyes than I had seen since she came in.

"We took it to George over at Byte Me." Byte Me was the local computer repair and maintenance shop. "He took the hard drive out and plugged it into another computer. He got pretty much all the data off."

Her head came up. "They can do that?"

"Unless it's encrypted. Then I think it's a bigger problem." Dad hadn't encrypted anything. Like I said, open book.

"Thanks, Desiree. That's a big help." She tried to smile, but it wasn't working too well.

"No problem." I stood in the doorway as she got into her car and drove off.

*   *   *

I placed all the orders for Rosemarie's choices. Then I unbundled the suit and shoes and all the rest from the clump Rosemarie had shoved at me. The shoes needed shining. The shirt needed ironing. The suit totally needed dry cleaning. I sighed and started going through the pockets and putting the items I found on the counter. I'd put them in an envelope for Rosemarie and give them back to her later. You never knew what someone might have an emotional attachment to, and you could hardly blame her for not having the emotional where-withal to go through his pockets herself. In this case, I was pretty sure it was all garbage or close to it. A paper clip. Three pennies and a nickel. A receipt from the Cold Clutch Canyon Café (named best café in Verbena by the *Verbena Free Press* five years running!), and a crumpled-up cellophane wrapper. I smoothed the receipt out flat and then did the same to the wrapper, which is when I noticed the sticker on it.

Professor Moonbeam's Dispensary and Bakery.

I gave the wrapper a sniff. I knew that smell. Since when had Alan Brewer been into weed? Don't get me wrong. Lots of people smoke marijuana. Or vape it. Or consume it in edibles. They always have. At least, they have since the late sixties. Alan and Rosemarie were of the ages where they definitely would have tried marijuana in high school or college at about the same time they tried beer. It was a rite of passage. Something that people did.

It wasn't like it was hard to get now either. There were doctors around who would give people a medical mari-juana card for just about anything. All you had to do was walk into their clinic and say you were anxious. Or your back hurt. Or there was a history of glaucoma in your fam-ily. Boom. A medical marijuana card would be yours.

After the last election, you didn't even need that anymore. Possessing small amounts of marijuana was perfectly legal. But just because it was legal didn't mean that everyone approved, though. Banks were notoriously fussy about their employees. I happened to know from a story I did on bank tellers that a lot of banks drug tested their employees. Would Alan risk his job for a quick high? It didn't seem likely. So where did the wrapper come from? Whose was it?

I put all the items in an envelope to give to Rosemarie later and then went down to the basement to let Uncle Joey know the plans that had been made. When we were done, he put his hand on my shoulder. "You did a good job, Desiree. I know that wasn't easy."

I felt tears prick at the back of my eyelids and rubbed them away. After the mess I'd made of Delia Burns's funeral, it was good to know I'd done something right. "Thanks, Uncle Joey."

"Your dad would be proud."

It had been a while since I felt like anything I was doing would have made him proud. "You think so?"

He patted me on the back with his huge paw of a hand. "I know so."

I hauled myself up to the top floor to check on Donna. She was stretched out on the old blue couch with an afghan that Mom had made over her legs. I opened the curtains over the window and coughed at the dust that rose up. "How's it going?" I probably didn't need to ask. She'd managed to crochet three quarters of a baby blanket in the time she'd been confined to the couch. Her fingers moved so fast that the hook was a blur. My sister wasn't used to sitting still.

"I'm bored." She set the yarn down in her lap. "What's happening downstairs?"

"I helped Rosemarie make arrangements for Alan." I lifted her feet and sat down on the couch, putting her feet in my lap. If it was good enough for Greg, it was good enough for me.

"Ouch. How bad was it?" She had the good grace to look sad for me.

"Pretty much as awful and awkward as you're imagining right now, but it's done." I rubbed her feet.

"I will give you exactly ten minutes to stop that." She moaned a little. "How was Rosemarie?"

"I'll give you two minutes, and Rosemarie was pretty much exactly the way you'd expect her to be. Sad. Subdued. A little angry. Do you need anything else?" I asked.

She gestured around her. She had tea, an apple, two magazines and one novel, a box of tissues, and about five skeins of yarn in various shades of pink, yellow, and baby blue. "What more could I possibly need?"

"I have no idea. You're pregnant. Aren't you supposed to want pickles and ice cream or something like that?" None of my friends had started to procreate. Donna was the first. I wasn't really sure what to expect. Maybe I should have read that book she kept by her side like a bible.

"Aren't you supposed to have cultural references more current than the 1950s?" she countered. "Oh, thanks for this, by the way." She held up something.

"For what?"

"This?" She opened her palm. In it was a charm for a bracelet. It was a little baby crib.

"Cute, but why are you thanking me?"

"Greg said he found it on the porch. I assumed you'd gotten it and put it there for me." She leaned forward to pat my arm. "It's really sweet of you. It's exactly the charm that Dad would have gotten me. I hadn't even known how much I wanted it until I saw it."

"Uh, Donna, I'm glad you like it, but I didn't get it." I went across the hall to my room and got the hiking boot charm I'd found on my car out at the Cold Clutch Canyon trailhead and came back to the family room. "I found this on my car when I came back from a hike."

Donna took it from me and turned it over in her hand.

"Who do you think is leaving them? Uncle Joey?" she suggested, but she started shaking her head before I could even begin to disagree with her. "No, he'd just give it to us. He wouldn't hide them around like weird little Easter eggs."

"What if . . ." I hesitated to say what I was about to say. "What if it's a ghost thing? Like a communication from beyond the grave?"

Donna sank back on the couch and made a face at me. "I can't think of two people less likely to buy into a ghost story than you and me. If there were such a thing as ghosts, this place would be crawling with them. Don't even start down that path. We'll go out of our ever-loving minds."

I sighed. "Fine, but it's weird."

"Weird, but not woo-woo," she agreed. "What's on deck for now?"

"I have the Tennant viewing." I stretched my arms over my head, hoping to release some of my tension.

Donna winced. "You sure you can handle it?"

I made a face at her. "Yes, I can. Oh, and I need to deposit some money at the bank. Rosemarie paid us in cash." I held up the envelope.

Donna's nose wrinkled. "In moldy cash?"

"She said she'd found it in their safe at home with their wills." I shrugged.

Chapter Nine

I pulled on my work clothes. I won't lie. They made me sigh. I felt so beige in them. Of course, I was supposed to be beige in them. I was supposed to melt into the background, invisible until someone needed me. Even then, I was supposed to be unobtrusive.

Donna was right about this funeral being a tough one. It was definitely harder than Miss Delia's. I had been fond of Miss Delia and would miss her and the way she would smack me on the arm if she thought I looked good. She saw me right before I went to junior prom and left a bruise. I don't think I've ever felt prettier. I knew, however, that Miss Delia had had a good run. So had Mr. Murray. In fact, his run had been so good and long, it had nearly taken his daughter with him.

I didn't feel the same way about Michael Tennant. It had been an accident, a stupid accident. A slip and fall off a ladder while cleaning out the gutters. Head cracked on the walkway. At first, he stood up and walked around and laughed about it. Then, according to his wife, he started speaking in garbled sentences. She called 9-1-1, but he'd slipped into a coma before they arrived.

He'd never woken up.

Subdural hematoma. Bleeding in the brain. There had been two surgeries to try to relieve the pressure, but nothing had worked. He was gone, leaving his wife and two kids behind, shocked and stunned. I had lost my dad too soon, but I'd had him for close to two decades more than Michael Tennant's kids had. My heart ached for them.

"You have to take yourself out of the equation," Donna had counseled me before I met with them. "This is not about you. It's about them."

I'd tried my best to keep that first and foremost in my mind. This was about their loss, not mine. I hoped my empathy helped rather than hurt.

I checked to make sure Mr. Tennant's makeup still looked good. The light in the Magnolia Room was slightly different than it was downstairs, and sometimes that required some adjustment, but he looked great. Just the right amount of color in his cheeks and lips. Mouth not smiling, but not frowning either. That his head looked round was a minor miracle performed by Uncle Joey and the internal workings of this particular casket that allowed you to tilt the body a bit. The original fall plus the subsequent surgeries hadn't left a pretty picture on the back of his head. In fact, it looked a little like a bad home-ec quilt pieced together from mismatched fabric. Not anymore, though. Not that anyone was going to see the back of Mr. Tennant's head unless they flipped him over in the casket—something we definitely frown upon at Turner Family Funeral Home. Uncle Joey never cared that no one would know what an artist he was, however. People would come, look at Mr. Tennant, be sad, and leave. They'd never know what he could have looked like or how horrific his injuries had been. I hoped he'd be able to work a similar miracle for Alan Brewer.

More and more people opted for cremation these days with a memorial service afterward whenever it was convenient. We never tried to dissuade them from that. There are a lot of arguments to be made for it. It gives people time to get there since so many of us are scattered about. The cremains can go nearly anywhere. You don't have to pay for a plot in a cemetery. There was also, however, an argument to be made for people saying a final good-bye to their loved ones with the loved ones as intact as we could make them. It brings a sense of closure. The grief may never fully go away, but at least you got to say good-bye properly.

The widow and her two daughters came into the chapel. I walked over to them and stood for a second. "Ms. Tennant, Jackie, and Jennifer, I am so very sorry for your loss. Would you like to take your seats?" I gestured to the front of the room, where the first row was reserved for family.

"Can we . . . can we see him?" Ms. Tennant asked, sounding timid. She nodded toward the girls, asking the unspoken question about whether it was safe for them to see their father.

I took her hand and nodded. "Of course." I led them to the front of the room, where he lay in the Esquire casket (medium range, gasket seal, metal fittings).

She looked in and turned away abruptly, holding a tissue to her eyes.

"Is everything okay?" I asked, worried for a moment that we'd done something wrong—made him too pink or too brown or parted his hair wrong.

"Yes. Yes. I was worried that he'd . . . that he wouldn't look like him. With the accident and . . ." Her words trailed off.

Apparently Uncle Joey's work was appreciated after all. "I understand."

She reached in and rested her hand briefly on his shoulder, then moved away to let the two girls walk up. Their eyes were so big in their heads, it seemed they had no other features. Holding hands, they approached the casket. The little one also reached in like her mother had, but she took his hand and tucked something inside. "Good-bye, Daddy," she whispered and then turned and ran to her mother. The older girl patted his hand and then returned to her mother, but at a more stately pace. "Could we, uh, use your restroom?" Ms. Tennant asked.

"Of course." I ushered them back out into the lobby and pointed the way. Once they were gone, I went back into the Magnolia Room to see what little Jennifer had slipped into her father's hand. I hadn't wanted to say anything until I knew what it was. It was a piece of paper, folded over and over and over into a small square. I carefully undid the folds and smoothed out the creases. It was a drawing. Not quite stick figures, but close. A man holding the hand of a little girl with a big yellow sun shining overhead and flowers around their feet. I knew exactly how she felt. I carefully refolded the drawing and tucked it back into Mr. Tennant's hand. I had a feeling that he'd want to hold on to something like that for as long as he could.

There's something about the ritual of saying good-bye that allows us to move on in peace. I doubted that Jennifer would ever forget her daddy or that she would ever not be sad about losing him too soon. I hoped that what we did that day would allow her to not be tormented by those memories, to not feel like she had unfinished business.

We'd eventually had a memorial service for Dad. We'd had everything that we had for Mr. Tennant. The big blown-up portrait, the flowers, the music, the readings. We hadn't had the body, though. We hadn't had him here. We hadn't borne witness to the truth and finality of his passing. Maybe that's why I'd had such a hard time moving on; maybe that's why I still felt so unsettled. Donna didn't seem to have the same problem, nor did Uncle Joey. It was just me who seemed to keep this little candle of hope lit in her heart that, without his body, maybe it wasn't true.

Ms. Tennant and her daughters came back in, and I seated them in front. Olive, Henrietta, and Grace arrived and took their usual spots. "Are you okay, dear?" Grace asked as I helped them fold up and stow their walkers.

"Of course," I said. "Why?"

"Oh, nothing," she said, looking over at Henrietta.

Henrietta snorted. "You look terrible."

My hand went up to my face as if I could feel the terrible on it. "I do?"

"Not terrible. Sad." Olive gave Henrietta a dirty look. "Of course she looks sad, you old biddy. This has to remind her of her father's memorial service. Plus there's Kyle . . ."

"He was like a second father to her, you know," Grace said, tapping Henrietta's knee.

"He's not dead," I said. "Kyle's fine."

"As fine as you can be in a jail cell," Henrietta said.

"He won't be there for long. He's innocent." I took her walker from her.

Henrietta sniffed. "Some people might think he'd done the town a favor."

I stopped. "What do you mean?"

"I mean that Alan was always looking for an angle. Even when he was a child. Always trying to figure out how to get that extra piece of candy or get ahead of someone else without doing the work," she said. "Not exactly anyone's favorite type of person."

Olive smacked Henrietta's arm with a rolled-up program. "Don't speak ill of the dead."

A group of people walked in. I needed to go seat them, so I left my three regulars. What kind of man was Alan, anyway? Jasmine said that everybody hated bankers, but were there a few people who seemed to hate Alan especially?

How many people might have wanted Alan dead? How many had Luke investigated?

Chapter Ten

The Verbena Free Press

TUESDAY, JULY 16

Civic Center Reopens

The Verbena Civic Center has reopened after a two-month closure. A squirrel infestation caused significant wiring damage, and city officials opted to close the venue while rewiring the building. Call the city offices to reserve the center for functions of any kind.

I am the obituary writer for the Turner Family Funeral Home. We have a form the bereaved fill out, and from it I construct a few paragraphs about a person's life and who will miss them. I think Uncle Joey thought it would make me feel close to my old profession. Sweet, right? Unfortunately, it made me feel like an even bigger loser.

Obituary writing is pretty much the bottom of the barrel. No journalist actually writes obituaries anymore, unless the person who died was a big deal in some way or another. Mr. Murray had been sweet, but he wasn't a big enough deal to have a ready-to-go obituary in a file at the *Washington Post* or the *New York Times*. People like me, people who worked at funeral homes, wrote obituaries.

I glanced at my watch. It was four thirty. I could drop this off at the *Verbena Free Press* office and still get to the bank before it closed. When I entered the *Verbena Free Press* office, Rafe was on the phone. I gestured for him to hang up. He held up one finger to suggest I wait. The office looked more like a DMV than a newspaper, with a long counter running the length of the room and separating the entrance from the rest of the space.

I rolled my eyes but decided to give him a second. I had a few things I wanted to say to him. When he got off the phone, I said, "I have obituaries for Mr. Rahimi, Mr. Tennant, and Mr. Murray."

"Thanks. You could have e-mailed them, though. Is there something else?" he asked, an altogether too cocky grin on his face.

I took a deep breath to get my nerve up to say what I'd really come in to say. "Yeah, now that you mention it, I do. Stop putting me in the paper."

He leaned back in his chair and put his feet up on his desk and stroked his chin. "I'll stop as soon as you stop doing newsworthy things."

No way was he going to turn this back on me. "That's the thing. I'm not doing anything newsworthy. I'm saying, 'No comment.' I'm doing my job at my family's business. You're working me into stories for no good reason." My voice rose. I took another deep breath to calm myself. Getting hysterical was not going to help. "I'm not news."

"I beg to differ." He brought his chair down with a bang. "Every interesting thing that has happened in this town since you came back has had some kind of connection with you."

"That's not true." It wasn't, was it?

"Let's see. You come home and fistfights start breaking out at funerals and close family friends get arrested for murder. I only put you in when there's a connection to you. Your name doesn't appear once in the article about the reopening of the Civic Center, although maybe I just haven't figured out a connection between you and the squirrel infestation." He shrugged. "Besides, whether or not it's true, it's not your call now, is it? You know that. People don't get to choose when they're newsworthy and when they're not. Not unless you want to get back into the news biz and help make those decisions. Wanna come to work here at the *Free Press*?"

Something fluttered in my chest. Becoming a reporter at the *Verbena Free Press* would be like starting all over again at the bottom of the ladder I'd worked so hard to climb. But not becoming a reporter anywhere again would be like refusing to climb the ladder at all. I'd screwed up. I knew that. I had to pay the price like anybody else. Maybe starting from that bottom rung was the price to return to the career I'd loved. Then another thought struck me. Good reporters never accept anything at face value. He had to have an angle. "Why? What would you get out of having me on staff here?"

"You know the people. You know the gossip. You know the business, and you have the chops." He got up and sauntered over to the counter, then gestured around at the empty office. "I could use some help too."

"My family needs me right now," I said. Did I want to get back into the news biz? I wasn't even sure anymore. The way I'd departed had left a sour taste in my mouth.

I'd spent the six years since I'd graduated from college climbing the reporter ranks in Los Angeles. I'd done the police beat. I'd written up city council meetings. I'd been the person they sent out in the rainstorm to be filmed getting wet in the rain so we could tell people it was raining outside. I'd finally—finally!—gotten the opportunity to do some stories on my own, and I'd stumbled on a whopper.

A local nursing home was bilking thousands of dollars from senior citizens, double billing for procedures, billing for brand-name drugs but using generics. That kind of thing. I'd gotten an anonymous call telling me what to look for, and I'd found plenty. I'd investigated and was convinced I had something that would get me a Pulitzer. I pitched the story. Not only did the station chief not take it, but suddenly I was back to being the person who got sent to stand out in the rain. It took me weeks to find out why. Turned out our station chief was married to the niece of the nursing home owner.

That's when I got angry. I hadn't decided what to do yet with that anger when I was sent out with a camera crew to stand on the edge of a cliff to show people how windy it was. Jeff, my cameraman, jokingly said, "So who did you piss off to start getting sent out here again?"

I told him. I told him the whole story. Then I did an imitation of the station chief saying, "I hate old people. Old people smell funny. Who cares if someone rips them off? Old people suck."

Neither of us realized that my mic was hot and that the anchor had cut to me a little earlier than we'd expected. My anti–old people rant went out live with no context.

Senior citizens' rights groups were demanding I be fired before I even got back to the station. By the time I made it clear that I was mocking someone who felt that way, it was too late. The video had gone viral. Last time I checked, the YouTube clip had over three million hits. There were memes. Since the station chief knew what I was really talking about, I'd been fired. Thank goodness my dad had already disappeared; at least he didn't have to see me humiliate myself. The other silver lining? The state started to investigate, and the nursing home owner was sanctioned and fined.

"I don't think I'm ready for a return to journalism," I told Rafe.

"Fine, but the offer stands for the moment. That nursing home story was righteous. Who knows what kinds of things are going on around here that need to be uncovered? If the time comes that your family doesn't need you so much anymore, come here and work for me." He grinned.

"For you? Not with you?" I asked.

"Semantics." He shrugged. "I could use some help on feature stuff—you know, restaurants reviews, recipes, community happenings. That Fire Festival thing, for instance. What the heck is that, anyway? How many festivals do you people have?"

Recipes? Community happenings? I'd been on the road to become a true investigative journalist. Then there was that whole "you people" thing. He'd called the town "you people." He'd set himself up as an outsider, and that's how he'd stay. With that kind of attitude he wouldn't last long. He'd never be able to do what he was asking me to do. He did have a point, though. We Verbenaites shut down Main Street about once a month to celebrate everything from almonds to zucchinis. "We have as many as we want," I said. "But the Fire Festival is definitely the crown jewel of the festival season."

"And why do we celebrate fire?" he asked, reminding me way too much of hearing the four questions asked at a Passover Seder I'd attended years ago.

"We don't celebrate fire in general. We celebrate a specific fire," I said. "The fire of 1913."

"Of course. Who wouldn't want to celebrate the fire of 1913? What was so special about that one?" he asked.

"It burned down pretty much the whole town," I said. "What there was of it back then, at least."

He shook his head. "And you *celebrate* it?"

"Not the fire so much as what happened afterward." I gestured around toward the town. "We rebuilt. From the ashes, we rose. Everyone chipped in. Everyone worked. It's a symbol of what this community is about." It was why anyone who referred to the residents of the town as "you people" would never understand the first thing about what motivated people and what they'd find important. "Look around at the architecture downtown. It's all this fantastic early art deco stuff because it was all built at about the same time."

"See? You know this stuff. You care about this stuff. Come write about this stuff." He pressed his hands together into a prayer position.

I did care about that stuff. It did make my heart pump faster. "I'll think about it. Until then, leave me out of the news, okay?"

He leaned in so our heads were nearly touching. He smelled like fresh-cut grass, clean and sharp. "No can do. You're news if I say you're news." He grinned wider. Then he sniffed the air. "Do you have dirt in your purse?"

Rosemarie's cash. I'd been carrying it around long enough that I couldn't smell it anymore. Apparently, other people could. "No," I said, sliding my purse around toward my back.

I left the newspaper office feeling confused. I didn't like the little flutter in my chest that had happened when Rafe talked to me about working at the newspaper, or maybe it was just because he always seemed to stand too darn close to me. I marched over to the Verbena Union Bank, took my place in line, and hoped nobody else could smell the cash in my purse. Dirty money, indeed.

The Verbena Union Bank was not one of the venerable old buildings of Verbena. It was, in my opinion, a bit of an eyesore. One of those awful 1970s American Brutalism concrete buildings. It was hard and sharp and without decoration. It reminded me of a prison. Inside, however, it was nice and cool. The air conditioning felt good on my flushed face. Cubicles lined one set of walls, tellers were on another. There were two actual offices against the back wall. One of them still had Alan's name on the door. He, of course, wasn't in it. His assistant, Johanna, was sorting through the papers on his desk and talking on the phone.

I headed toward the office, thinking I could offer my condolences, and her voice rose.

"How the heck should I know?" she demanded. "He did what he wanted. Now I'm here having to sort through all the mess."

She listened for a moment, then said, "I don't think any of it is technically illegal."

I paused. She had to be talking about Alan. What had he been up to? Something that would get the bank in trouble? Something unethical that could hurt people in the community? I held my breath.

With the hand that wasn't holding the receiver, she covered her face. "Yes. Of course, I'll keep looking." She hung up and noticed me in the doorway. "Can I help you, Desiree?"

I'd heard that tone before. It was the one people used when they didn't want to help you at all. It was the one that meant they'd rather you get the heck out of there. "No. I hadn't gotten a chance to tell you how sorry I am about Alan."

She leaned back in the big office chair. "Oh, yes. Well, thank you. It's been quite a shock."

"I can imagine," I said, taking a tentative step into the office. "It's so hard when things happen suddenly. No one has time to prepare or get anything in order."

She gestured at the desk, covered with file folders. "Don't I know it."

I stretched my neck just a little to see if I could read any of the file labels. They all seemed to be numbers, though. "Are there problems?"

Her eyes narrowed. I'd gone too far. "Nothing I can't handle. Is there anything else?"

I backed out. "No. That's all."

I heard the door click shut behind me as I made my way to the line for the teller. When it was my turn, I plunked the envelope of cash along with some checks onto the counter. "I'd like to deposit these into the Turner Family Funeral Home account."

The teller, a young man with spiked black hair and a ring in his eyebrow that didn't seem to go with his starched dress shirt and tie, picked them all up and wrinkled his nose.

"I know," I said. "The money smells funny. That's not a problem, is it?"

He laughed. "It isn't for the guys from over at the car wash. All their money smells like this."

"Really?" That seemed odd.

"Yeah. I figure it has to do with being near all those hoses and stuff." He counted out the bills, stamped the checks, and handed me a receipt.

"I thought these smelled more like dirt than damp," I said.

He shrugged. "Whatever. It's still gonna spend."

Exactly what I thought. "So," I said, "must be kind of weird around here with Alan gone."

The teller looked behind me. I looked too. Nobody had come in after me. I was the last of the line. Then he said, "If by weird you mean awesome, then yes."

I leaned forward. Maybe he knew what Johanna had been talking about on the phone. Could Alan have upset someone here enough that they might want to kill him? Money was right up there as a reason for people to kill. That and love. "So he wasn't a great boss?"

Pierced Eyebrow made a face. "He was one of those guys who was a stickler about everybody else following the rules but somehow felt they didn't apply to him. Like we all have to punch a time clock, but he waltzed in and out of here whenever he wanted. Johanna had to clean out the refrigerator in the break room every Friday, but he'd leave dirty dishes in the sink."

"So kind of a hypocrite?" I asked. If we killed all the hypocrites in the world, it'd be a pretty empty place. It didn't seem like enough of a reason to kill him.

"A hypocrite with a mean streak." He sorted the bills I'd given him into stacks. "He told anyone who argued with him that it was his bank and he'd run it how he pleased, and if we didn't like it, we knew where the door was." He laughed.

"Why is that funny?" I asked.

"Well, when we get vandalized, it's always the door that Alan used to point to that got messed with." He tapped the different piles of bills into neat stacks.

"Do you get vandalized a lot?" I asked.

"You could say that. Mainly spray paint and that kind of stuff, but once there was a decapitated Ken doll." He squinted up into the distance. "I think the last time was only about a week ago."

"What would they spray-paint?" I asked.

"Oh, stuff. Things like 'Die, Banker. Die.'"

Whoever it was had gotten their wish. The banker had died. I wondered if the vandal could have had a hand in it.

Chapter Eleven

Dad had always kept a stash of charms to give to Donna and me. Donna's comment about it being exactly like something Dad would give us made me wonder if that stash was still there. We'd looked through his things back when he disappeared, but I didn't remember seeing them. Maybe they were hidden some place we didn't look. We hadn't exactly been at our best when we'd gone through his things. We hadn't even been sure what we were looking for.

Back at home, I stood in front of the closed door to his room. I hadn't been in the room since a few days after his disappearance. I took a deep breath, blew it out, and turned the handle. The room on the other side was just the same as the last time I'd been in it, except it was now coated with dust, another by-product of living in a place that didn't get much rain.

But not everything was coated with the same amount of dust. There were some clear-ish spots on Dad's desk. I sat down in the chair in front of it. I pulled the top drawer open. Well, I tried to pull it open. It moved a few inches and then stuck. I rattled it a little. It still wouldn't open. I rattled it a little harder.

Nothing.

Something was jamming it. I crawled under the desk to see if I could find what was keeping it from opening and found a small key on a key ring. It had gotten wedged along the bottom edge of the drawer. With a combination of tugging on the key and wiggling the drawer, it finally came loose and fell into my hands.

The key ring had a logo and a name on it: Pluma Vista Storage. Someone had written a number on it with a Sharpie. I crawled out from underneath the desk and sat down in the chair again. Just because the key ring said Pluma Vista Storage didn't mean that the key was to a storage unit. It sure implied it, though, and the key was definitely the type that fit a padlock.

Why would Dad have needed a storage unit? Turner Family Funeral Home was big. There was a ton of space to store things. I should know. Pretty much all the belongings I'd amassed since leaving here were in a corner of the basement and there was still plenty of room.

I slid the key into my pocket and left the room. I walked down the hallway and across to where Donna was. "Did Dad ever mention anything to you about a storage space?"

She shook her head. "Why would he have one of those?"

"My question exactly." I pulled out the key. "I found this in his desk drawer."

Her eyes narrowed. "Why were you going through his desk drawers?"

I sat down on the floor next to the couch. "I was seeing if Dad was keeping a stash of those charms. I didn't remember seeing any, so I went looking."

"And instead you found a key?" she asked, her crochet hook slowing a tiny bit.

"Yeah. What do you think?" I had an uneasy feeling. Maybe our dad wasn't the open book we thought he was.

"I think that nearly everyone I know has a stash of miscellaneous keys around. It might not mean anything." She paused. "But we should probably double-check. Make sure there's nothing we're supposed to be dealing with."

"Yeah, that's what I was thinking," I said. It hadn't been, but it was as good an excuse as any to take a look inside it. It would have to wait, though. I had something more pressing to look into. Someone had written "Die, Banker. Die" on the door of the Verbena Union, and then the banker had died. Was there a connection? Had Luke Butler even bothered to look into it? I sincerely doubted it. He hadn't looked into anything once he found that gun in the pond. He'd slapped the cuffs on Kyle and washed his hands of the whole thing. Well, I wasn't afraid to get my hands dirty. In fact, I liked it.

I palmed the key and said, "Need anything?" to Donna.

She shook her head. "I'm fine."

Something in her tone of voice made me pause. "Are you sure? You sound a little puny." *Puny* had been one of our grandfather's words, he of the blessed heart attack. It encompassed everything from a head cold to a hangover.

She looked up from her crocheting and smiled. "Not in the least bit puny. Stop worrying."

"Okay. I'm right across the hall if you need me." I went back to my room. I dropped the key into the little heart-shaped bowl on my dresser and climbed onto the bed with my laptop.

My next step was to take a look at the police logs online. Most of the calls that the police department had gone out on would be listed there. It shouldn't take long to find out if the bank had reported the vandalism. I found the website and started coasting through the log. Someone had reported a possible intruder in the 300 block of Dove Lane. I frowned. That was Jasmine's street. There'd been a drunk and disorderly out on Highway 157. That was by the Green Owl Tavern and totally to be expected. One car broken into over on Plover Street and tools stolen from a shed on Kingfisher Avenue. Then I hit it: "Police respond to report of vandalism at Verbena Union Bank." Then there wasn't another mention. If any investigation followed, it wasn't showing up here.

It was something to follow up on. Something I could do to help clear Kyle's name. I called Lola and stretched while I listened to the phone ring. I'd been tensed up all day about the Tennant funeral. My jaw hurt from clenching my teeth. I really needed it to go as close to perfectly as it could. I didn't want to screw it up for so many reasons. I wanted their good-bye to be as good a memory for them as it could be, and I didn't want to disappoint Donna. Plus, I was getting a little tired of being a failure.

Finally Lola answered the phone. "How are you doing?" I asked.

"As well as can be expected." Her voice sounded small.

"I have a few questions for you. Do you feel up to it?" I pulled a pad of paper out of my desk drawer and found a pen.

"If you think it might help get Kyle out of jail, then I'm up for anything."

I smiled. That sounded more like the Lola I knew and loved. "Who knew you had a gun?"

She paused. "Nearly everyone. It's pretty common out here."

She was right about that. "Okay. How many people would know how to get into the house?"

"Pretty much anyone who tried the door. Kyle's terrible about locking it."

This wasn't getting me my list to help narrow people down. On the other hand, that meant that I wouldn't have to eliminate many suspects. "What about the gun cabinet? Would people have known where that was?"

"Anybody who'd ever been on the porch would have seen it. We mainly used the gun to kill rattlesnakes and things like that. It always made sense to keep it near the deck and outdoors. You wouldn't even have to come inside to see it. It's visible from the garden."

We hung up. My second call was to Carol Burston. "Hi, Carol. It's Desiree Turner. The other day when you were up at Cold Clutch, did you happen to see anybody hanging around my car?"

"Which day?" she asked.

I told her.

She thought for a moment. "Oh. Was that the day that the gray Element was there too?"

My pulse quickened. "Yes, it was. Do you know whose car it was?"

"No. It just struck me as funny. Your dad loved those cars. Swore by them. I always thought they were a little weird with those funky doors. So it was funny to see yours there with another one almost exactly like it. Why are you asking?"

"Nothing, really. Someone left something on the car. Nothing bad. A little gift. I was trying to figure out who it was so I could thank them."

"Sorry. Didn't see a person. Just the car."

We hung up. I'd written nothing down on my notepad. I knew from my reporting days that there were always dead ends, threads you'd follow that ended up leading nowhere, connections that ended up being coincidences. This felt like the opposite of that. Every avenue I walked down seemed to open up to more avenues. I needed to narrow things down.

Lots of people hated Alan. I'd have to start looking at them one at a time.

Chapter Twelve

The Verbena Free Press

WEDNESDAY, JULY 17

Funeral Services Scheduled for Murder Victim

A viewing and funeral services have been scheduled for Alan Brewer. Mr. Brewer died on Saturday from a gunshot wound. His neighbor, Kyle Hansen, is currently awaiting arraignment in relation to that crime.

The viewing will be held at the Turner Family Funeral Home. It will be followed by a graveside service at Lawn of Heaven Cemetery and then a reception and celebration of life at the Civic Center in downtown Verbena.

Contact Assistant Funeral Director Desiree Turner at Turner Family Funeral Home with questions or concerns at 555-2489.

Alan Brewer's viewing was the biggest event I ever remember seeing at Turner Family Funeral Home, bigger even than Dad's memorial service. It was beyond standing room only. People spilled out into the lobby and into the front lawn. I hesitate to call them all mourners.

There were definitely a few who seemed sad, but the notoriety of his death had drawn quite a few people who probably normally wouldn't attend this kind of service. Olive, Henrietta, and Grace were outraged. Luckily, they had arrived early, or I probably wouldn't have been able to save them their customary seats.

"Who are all these people, Desiree?" Grace whispered to me.

"People here to say good-bye to Alan?" I suggested. "People here to comfort Rosemarie in this difficult time?"

She made a disgusted noise in the back of her throat. "Please! Most of these people wouldn't have recognized Alan if they'd seen him walking down the street. A bunch of lookie-loos. They're here because it's murder." I felt like there was some hypocrisy in there somewhere but decided not to pursue it.

"Who doesn't like a murder?" Henrietta asked.

"The victim?" I suggested.

That got a snort from Henrietta, which then turned into a coughing fit. After I brought her a glass of water—I didn't want her to turn into another customer while we still had a viewing going on—I continued to circulate, making sure that everything was being done the way Rosemarie had wanted.

Uncle Joey had done an amazing job on Alan's forehead. If you looked at it at the right (or possibly wrong) angle, you could see a depression, but you certainly would never guess that it had been a bullet hole. He was just the right amount of pink, and his hair looked terrific. People filed by, murmuring to each other. It didn't seem like anybody would be reaching in or doing anything like that, but I kept an eye on how things were going anyway. People could surprise you.

I saw one woman slide out her phone and take a quick, sneaky picture of Alan in the casket. I might not have noticed if I hadn't used the same technique a time or two when I was working as a reporter. A quick slip of the phone out of the pocket, never raise it higher than your waist, click off a bunch of shots, and hope what you want is framed in the photo. I started toward her to make sure she didn't get even more inappropriate, but she'd moved on by the time I made my way through the crowd to her. She certainly didn't look like someone who would make a scene at a funeral. She looked like a nice little old lady. Short white hair. Rockport shoes. It made me uneasy, though. It was one step on that slippery slope. Once you got away with taking a photo of the corpse in the casket, you might get drunk at the reception and announce that you'd borne Alan's love child or try to swipe the pocket square from Alan's chest as some kind of grisly souvenir. It was a murder, and murder made people act in strange ways. That's part of what made murders so damn interesting.

Nothing else interesting happened at the viewing, though. The pallbearers lined up. I recognized the young man from the bank whom I'd nicknamed Pierced Eyebrow as well as a few other stalwarts of the business community. I was relieved. Everyone looked strong. I've occasionally been worried about the pallbearers collapsing on their way to the hearse, where Uncle Joey waits for them. Not this time, though.

After Alan was carried out, everyone else left and moved in the general direction of the Lawn of Heaven Cemetery except Olive, Henrietta, and Grace. The ground was too uneven for them anymore.

The graveside service went smoothly. Pastor Campbell said his usual stuff about heaven and read the usual psalm. I didn't think Alan and Rosemarie were big churchgoers, and he didn't appear to know them well. He did a fine job anyway. It was all a little generic but appropriate.

Then everyone left for the reception Rosemarie was holding at the Civic Center. I stayed to make sure everything continued to go smoothly. By myself. Nobody becomes an assistant funeral director to make friends. People don't want to come to see you when this is your profession. If they're coming to see you, something sad has happened. Someone with whom they have a connection, whether good or bad, is gone. While your heart may be filled with love and respect for humanity, it's a lonely job. I didn't mind.

Verbenaites have been buried at Lawn of Heaven for decades. The cemetery was tied to the town's history. My great-grandpa, founder of Turner Family Funeral Home, was buried here. He came to Verbena, California, in the late 1800s. Post–gold rush, but only just. He'd traveled west from Missouri with an actual wagon train. On the way, he'd become pretty handy with making repairs and, sadly, at burying bodies. When he got to Verbena, nobody was making caskets and burying people. He set up shop on Blackbird Street, married Alta Osgood, the schoolmistress—Dad said Donna and I got our bookish side from her—and had one son, my grandfather. Grandpa took over and then passed the home down to my father and my uncle.

Piero Tappiano, founder of Tappiano's winery, was buried here too. He'd come about the same time as my great-grandfather. He'd started out as a field hand on a wheat farm. Then he married his boss's daughter and started planting whatever he wanted, including grapes. The first wine he'd made had been for family and friends, but word had spread. Pretty soon he'd stopped planting wheat at all.

If you came on Memorial Day or Veteran's Day, you'd see flags waving all around the cemetery on the graves of the many Verbenaites who had served. In a few days, the high school history club would place flowers on the graves of the victims of the 1913 fire.

My mother was here. My dad's plot—although, of course, not my dad—was here. It struck me as a little ironic that a person who dedicated his life to helping others dispose of their earthly remains couldn't have his disposed of because we didn't know where they were.

Even with all that connection to the town and its history, there's a special kind of loneliness after the ceremony is over and everyone has left and you're the one staying to make sure the last details are done correctly.

Or, at least, there usually is.

The gravediggers finished with Alan's grave. They lowered the casket into the ground, removed the Astroturf that had covered the mounds of dirt, and filled the grave back in. They left, and the peculiarly solitary feeling of an empty cemetery returned. I leaned against the tree, letting its strength seep into my bones while sheltering in its shade. I'm not sure how long I stood there, but it was long enough for the solitary feeling to change to one of serenity. It was nice. I needed a little more serenity in my life.

Actually, I needed a lot more serenity.

I was just about to leave when movement caught my eye. Marie Ruiz from the Cut 'n' Curl was making her way across the soft ground to Alan's newly filled-in burial

site. Marie was a good-looking woman in her early for-
ties. Blonde and busty with creamy skin, she was a great
advertisement for her own services. I didn't remember
her being at the viewing or the service, but it had been
really crowded. She stomped across the grass, a look of
determination on her face. I was about to call out to her,
to let her know that most of the mourners had already
gone to the Civic Center, when she spat on the grave and
said, "And stay down."

She turned and stomped away.

So much for serenity, but on the other hand, I'd found
someone specific who clearly hated Alan a lot.

Chapter Thirteen

The Civic Center wasn't exactly elegant. It was a much newer addition to the town than the buildings that went up right after the fire. It had that seventies feel to it like the bank. It was a square box of a building with tile floors and squinty little windows. No beautiful arches. No clay tiles. No brick details. It was, however, well air-conditioned, had easy parking, and had apparently resolved its squirrel issue. Rosemarie had rented the newly reopened main hall for the wake. While we were all at the graveside, the caterers had set up the portrait and the guest book from the funeral home. I stopped in mainly as a courtesy. My work was done. I parked my car in the corner of the lot in a shaded spot and walked toward the building.

I slipped into the room, staying to the edges, to make sure the caterers had set up the portrait and guest book appropriately. I shouldn't have worried. Rosemarie had hired Susan from Easy as Pie Caterers. Susan was a pro. She'd no sooner mess up a wake than become a bikini model, and she liked her own pie a little too much for that. Bikinis are overrated anyway. Pie, however, is always good.

Chairs had been set up in groupings around round tables draped with simple white cloths. Food was on long tables around the edges of the room, and the bar (wine and beer only) was over in the corner. Classical music was being piped in to the room. It sounded Mozart-y to me, but I wasn't sure. I circulated briefly around the room as I'd seen my dad do before. I checked in with Rosemarie to see if she needed anything.

She sat at a table with three other women. Someone had put a glass of wine in her hand, and she was sipping at it absently. At the very least, it had brought some color to her milky pale cheeks. A plate with a tea sandwich and some cookies sat at her elbow untouched. I was glad to see that someone had made sure to get her some food and drink and that she had some people to support her. She'd been alone every time I'd seen her since Alan died. No one should have to go through burying a spouse alone. "I wanted to check to see if you needed anything else from me, Rosemarie," I said.

"No," she said. "Thanks, but I think we've got it from here."

"Okay, then. Let me know if that changes." I put my hand over hers briefly.

She looked at my hand and then back up at me as if she'd just realized I was there. "Oh, Desiree. Thanks for that information about the passwords. It really helped."

"No problem, Rosemarie."

I did a quick survey of the room to see if there was anyone else I wanted or needed to talk to or anyone I needed to guide away. Marie Ruiz was not there. My sneaky paparazzi wasn't either. A lot of other people were, though. Alan might not have been well liked, but he was apparently prominent enough that people felt they had to come to pay their respects.

People from the bank gathered around one table. I recognized Johanna, the teller who'd helped me the day before, and Sophie Byrd, another teller. My teller friend leaned over and whispered something to Sophie, who tried to stifle a laugh. Luckily, the buzz of people talking in the room was mainly enough to mask it, although Johanna saw it and gave them both a big old dose of side eye for it. The two tellers exchanged a glance, and Sophie giggled again.

The business community had definitely turned out for Alan, which made sense. He had been pretty active in the Verbena Downtown Business Association (or VDBA, as it was known). They were ranged around the room. I saw Monique, who was using a napkin to carefully wipe the dirt from the spike of one of her high heels. People always forgot how spongy the ground at the cemetery could be. Wedge heels were always a better choice. Or slides. I thought I saw a flash of red sole but then decided I must have been mistaken. No way a waitress at Cold Clutch was wearing Louboutins, even with the extra moonlighting at Tappiano's in the evenings. Even a good knock-off would have set her back quite a bit. No wonder she was cleaning them so carefully.

None of that surprised me. The presence of Christine Brewer, however, did surprise me. Not many ex-wives attended funeral services. I hadn't thought they were on such good terms. I especially thought Christine and Rosemarie weren't on good terms, what with Rosemarie's time with Alan overlapping his time with Christine by quite a bit. Yet there she was with a pile of crumpled tissues in front of her. I supposed Alan couldn't be all bad if his ex-wife was mourning him, but then I passed behind the table close enough to hear her saying, "I just always thought I'd be able to get more money from him. Now that's never going to happen."

So not exactly mourning him, just his passing.

"How's it going, Desiree?" a voice at my elbow asked.

I jumped. It was my job at these things to ask how people were doing, not for people to ask me. I turned. Rafe. Of course. "Fine, I think. Alan got a good turnout."

"He did. Befitting a citizen as prominent as him." Rafe nodded.

"You're not here to pay respects, are you?" I asked.

He shrugged. "As much as a lot of these people are. You really think he'd have a crowd like this if he hadn't been murdered? Well, that and the last time his widow attended a funeral, a fistfight broke out. Everyone wants to make sure they don't miss anything."

"You included?" I asked with raised eyebrows.

He smiled. "Of course."

At least he didn't have his camera out. Then a thought occurred to me. "You didn't send someone into the viewing to take pictures of Alan in his casket, did you?"

To his credit, he turned a little green. "That is disgusting."

"Yeah, but you and I both know that our profession is more than occasionally a little disgusting," I pointed out.

"I didn't think we shared a profession anymore." He gestured at the room. "I thought this was your gig these days."

My cheeks got hot. "It is. And one of my jobs is to maintain the privacy and dignity of our clients even if they're murdered, so if I find out you sent that woman in to take a photo of Alan in his casket, I will make sure everyone in town knows it was you."

He held up his hands in front of him. "I get why you'd be suspicious of me, Desiree. I'm not saying I'm above doing something like that, even if it does turn my stomach. I do, however, know my audience. The readers of the *Verbena Free Press* would be every bit as horrified as you seem to be if I printed a photo like that."

He was right. We were a small town, and we had our noses deep in each other's business, but there were limits. The lines may not be very well defined, but I was pretty sure snapping photos of dead people while paying respects was far, far on the other side of what Verbena considered good behavior. "Fine," I grumbled. "Let me know if you hear anything about a photo like that, though, okay?"

"Will do." He hesitated. "Anything interesting you can tell me from having dealt with the widow?"

"Something for you to print?" I asked.

He nodded.

"No comment."

Suddenly, Nate was at my elbow. "Everything okay here, Desiree?" he asked.

I looked back and forth between Rafe and Nate, who both seemed to be trying to pull themselves up beyond their full heights. "I'm fine," I said.

"I'll be on my way," Rafe said. "Stories to file and all that."

We watched him walk away. "I don't like that guy. I'm not sure why, but I definitely don't like him." He paused and looked around. "Does it seem awfully . . . blonde in here to you?"

Nate had always been a little faster to notice the ethnic makeup of a crowd than I had, but this one hadn't struck me as particularly white. It had seemed more like Verbena itself. A mishmash. Mainly white, maybe, but with a healthy dose of other cultures and skin colors. Now I looked around. Maybe he was right. There were a lot of blondes. Trixie Warner from Bloom Where I'm Planted, Ella Keller from Fit 'n' Fine, and Mandy Smith from Count on Me all had the same honey-blonde hues in their hair as Rosemarie and, come to think of it, Christine. I shrugged. "Maybe. Maybe they all go to Marie at Cut 'n' Curl. That's her color. Probably just a coincidence, though, don't you think?"

"I think that's a lot of coincidental blonde."

Chapter Fourteen

I met Jasmine at Tappiano's. She was already settled at what I was starting to think of as our table, by the big plate glass window in front. Happy hour was dedicated to sparkling wine and smoked oysters. Apparently, I had died and gone to heaven. I was not alone in that thought. The room filled up as we sat with people's whose faces I knew from forever. Most waved. Some then whispered. Whatever. I turned my champagne flute around in slow circles on the table.

Jasmine dropped her hand on top of mine to stop me from fidgeting. "Don't do that. You're going to make the bubbles effervesce too quickly and it'll go flat. So how weird was it dealing with Rosemarie?"

I scrunched up my face and thought. "Medium weird. She's still too much in shock to be hard to deal with. She's barely putting one foot in front of the other." The vision of Rosemarie sitting staring at the plate in front of her as if she didn't know quite what to do with food flashed into my brain. She'd made Lola and Kyle miserable, but that didn't mean I didn't have sympathy for her situation now.

"Grief is hard." Jasmine took a sip.

"That's your professional opinion?" I asked. Maybe I'd get it cross-stitched onto a pillow for her birthday present. She'd like that. It would go well with the one she had that said, "Get Over It."

She nodded. "It's especially hard when the death is sudden. People have all kinds of unresolved issues."

Which reminded me of what I'd seen at the cemetery. "What's the deal between Marie Ruiz and Alan?" There was definitely something unresolved there.

"Why would there be any deal?" she asked.

"She waited until everyone left the cemetery and then spit on his grave." I was pretty sure that wasn't a casual thing.

"Seriously?" Jasmine's eyes went wide. "That's some real hatred there, like medieval put-his-head-on-a-pike kind of hatred."

"So probably not some casual disrespect, then? Not just a hatred for bankers in general?" I mulled that over. "No guesses?"

"I don't know her that well, except to know she's a way better stylist than anybody else over at Cut 'n' Curl. More than half the people that go there insist on going to her." She narrowed her eyes and looked at me. "You could use a cut, you know."

I knew she was right. I'd been enjoying not having to worry about my hair and my eyebrows and my nails. When you worked on air anywhere, you always needed to be groomed. But if you worked on air in Los Angeles? You better look salon fresh every second. Appearances mattered. Here at home in Verbena? Not so much. "How bad is it?"

She gave me a thorough once-over. "You need a trim, and a little wax wouldn't hurt your brow line one bit. You haven't gone total hippie, but I don't know how you're ever going to catch a man with split ends like that." She snorted.

"What about you? Do you go to her?" I asked. I'd always been jealous of Jasmine's curls. They seemed to spiral out of her head with just the right amount of bounce. My own dark hair was a touch on the thin side.

She fluffed her hair. "Yes. I do. But as you know, getting a man isn't on my agenda."

We'd been in junior high when Jasmine had confided in me that she liked girls way better than boys. It had taken me a little while to understand what she mean because I had still been in a phase where I thought boys were loud and stinky, and who wouldn't like girls better? Then I got it.

"Fine. I'll make an appointment before my hair gets worse. Maybe I can find out why she hated Alan so much." I ate another oyster. "Do you think Luke has even bothered to investigate if anybody besides Kyle could have shot Alan?" I took another sip of champagne.

Jasmine cocked her head to one side, making those curls bounce. "Why are you so sure that Kyle didn't do it?"

I sat upright and blinked. "Because he's Kyle. He wouldn't. Besides, he said he didn't."

"Isn't saying you're innocent pretty much de rigueur when you're accused of murder?" she asked.

"It's Kyle," I insisted. "I know him. I know he's innocent."

"Sure you know him. He was practically like a second dad to you. Do you really think you saw your own dad clearly?"

"What's that supposed to mean?" Dad had been easy to read. Always. Everything out in the open. Or at least, I thought everything had been. That key burned bright in my mind.

She held up her hands in front of her. "Nothing. That's kind of the point. We don't really see them as people. We think we know them, but we don't. I mean, just the other day I found out that my dad played saxophone in a jazz band in his youth."

I snorted. "Seriously? Your dad?" I loved Jasmine's dad. If I had a third dad, it would totally be him. But Mr. Rodrigues with a sax? I didn't think so.

"Yup. Found a photo stuffed in a drawer when I was looking for some paper clips and confronted him with it.

He was surprised that I didn't already know." She traced an invisible pattern on the bar. "As children, I think there are things we don't know about the adults in our lives because we don't want to know. We want them to be there for us, and beyond that, we don't really want to see them as people."

I sighed. "And if they're good parents, they don't force us to see them as people either, do they?"

"Nope."

We raised our glasses, clinked them together, and drank. "I need to go check on Donna. See you later?"

"Sure." Jasmine signaled for the check.

Mark Tappiano came out from behind the bar and spread his hands out. "It's all covered."

"That's so nice," I said. "But you didn't need to do that."

He furrowed his brow. "I didn't."

Jasmine got very still. "Then who paid for our drinks?" she asked.

Mark shrugged. "Somebody dropped this off earlier." He pulled an envelope out of his apron and handed it to Jasmine.

Jasmine pulled the contents out. She fanned four twenty-dollar bills out on the table along with a sheet of computer paper with a typed note on it:

Please use this money to pay for Ms. Jasmine Rodrigues's bill on her next visit. Keep the change.

"Who?" Jasmine asked. "Who dropped it off?"

Mark shifted on his feet a little. "I don't know. It was here when I got in. On the floor. I figured someone slipped it under the door. Should I not have used it?"

Jasmine held up her hand. "It's fine, but no. Don't use it. We'll pay our own bill."

"What should I do with the money?" he asked.

"Whatever you want. Give it to charity. Buy yourself something pretty. Just don't use it to cover anything of mine." Jasmine handed him a credit card.

"What's going on?" I asked after Mark walked away.

"I'm not sure." Jasmine chewed a little on her lower lip.

Now my eyes went wide. Jasmine didn't usually look anxious, but she sure did now. She shook her head. "Just a few weird things. There was that chocolate on my car. Then someone replaced the lightbulbs in my porch lights. I thought it might be my dad, but he said no."

I thought of the police report. "There was a report of a prowler in your neighborhood too."

She sat up straight. "When?"

"Last week."

She put her hand to her mouth. "That was around the time those lightbulbs got replaced. Wait. How did you know that?"

"I was looking at the police blotter."

"You are seriously weird, you know that?" She shook her head.

"What do you think it means?" I asked.

"I really don't know, but I think I'm going to have to find out." We both turned slowly on our seats to look out the window of Tappiano's as if her stalker might be standing right there. There was nothing to see but pajama man pulling into the Clean Green Car Wash in his truck coated with mud.

"Who is that guy anyway?" I pointed. Last time I'd been home, the view from this window had been of an open field. Granted, that field would have largely looked like a patch of dead weeds at the moment, but it had still been open space. Now there was a car wash—a car wash with two customers and about ten polo-shirted employees fussing over the cars. Even an eco-friendly car wash was a tough sell around here. A dusty car was a sign that you weren't wasting water.

Before Jasmine could answer, Luke Butler walked in. "Death Ray! Jasmine! How's it going?"

I sighed as he pulled a stool over to our table and sat. "Hello, Luke."

He smiled, then turned to see what we were looking at.

"When did that go up anyway?" I asked.

"Six or seven months ago? Something like that. Right before the Dollar General, but after the In-n-Out?" Jasmine said, sounding like Monique for a moment.

I didn't think a single new building had gone up when I'd lived here. Now businesses were popping up like moles in an arcade game. Verbena was growing. Too fast for my taste. "And who is that?"

"Who? There are like a dozen people over there." Jasmine pushed the glasses toward me.

"Yeah, but only one in pajamas." He kind of stood out.

"You mean Professor Moonbeam," he said.

Professor Moonbeam? Of the dispensary and bakery? Interesting.

Monique came up to the table, still tying her apron around her waist. She must have come straight from the funeral. Her eyes looked red as if she'd been crying.

Luke turned to Monique. "You got beer back there?" he asked.

Monique stared straight ahead out the window and didn't answer. I didn't blame her. Who ordered a beer at a wine bar? It was like ordering a hamburger at a Chinese restaurant.

"Yo, Monique, honey." Luke snapped his fingers, and she swung toward him. "Beer?"

"IPA okay?" she asked.

"More than okay." Luke swiveled away from her to give me his full attention.

"So who exactly is Professor Moonbeam?" I asked, still curious and quite happy to have the subject of conversation change. "Is he an actual professor?" Verbena was situated about twenty miles north of a University of

California campus and ten miles east of a state university. A lot of professors viewed it as a bedroom community.

Luke made a disgusted noise in the back of his throat. "He was. Once. In the ag school, believe it or not. He decided to channel all that knowledge to grow weed."

"It's legal now, you know," Jasmine pointed out.

Luke narrowed his eyes. "Barely. It still isn't legal on a federal level. It's a mess. A total quagmire."

Jasmine turned to me. "Luke doesn't approve of the marijuana business. He thinks marijuana is a gateway drug."

"It is!" He protested.

"I think wine coolers are the real gateway drug." They provided that first taste of an altered state. They got you hooked, and then you started looking for more. At least that's the way I remembered high school drinking. I swiveled back around on my barstool. "So what do you have against Mary Jane?"

"It attracts the wrong elements. Even if it's legal to possess it now, there are a lot of things around growing it and distributing it that aren't." Luke pressed his lips into a hard, straight line.

It pained me, but he was right. States were legalizing things left and right, but the Feds weren't. Even in states where possession and growing were legal, not every county or city official felt the same way about it. Yet the arc of history is long, and it bends toward legalization. "Don't you think it's just a matter of time before all of it is?"

"Probably, but until then, having a marijuana farm attracts a lot of people to the area that don't respect the law. If they don't respect one law, they probably won't respect another one," Luke said.

"What is it you think they're going to do?" I asked.

"For one thing, I think a lot of them carry firearms. Somebody's going to get shot," Luke said.

A shiver went up my spine. Somebody had already been shot. Somebody who had been walking around with a Professor Moonbeam's Dispensary and Bakery wrapper in his pants pocket. "You wouldn't arrest anyone for using, though, would you?"

He shook his head. "It's not illegal. There's nothing to arrest them for."

"So just having been a customer wouldn't be enough to get you in trouble?" I asked. That wrapper in Alan's pocket didn't indicate anything more incriminating than us having a glass of wine then, as long as the bank didn't have a no-tolerance drug policy.

He looked at me hard. "No. I can't see how it would. Why?"

I shrugged. I wasn't sure if it meant anything yet. Probably just another dead end. "Nothing."

"I don't think you're going to be able to stop any of this," Jasmine said. "It's going to be as respectable and accepted as drinking in a few years. People will have pyramids of joints at weddings next to the champagne fountains."

Luke said, "It might be legal, but I don't like anything associated with the drug trade in my town."

"Your town?" I snorted. "Since when is Verbena *your* town?"

"Since forever." He cocked his head. "Don't tell me you don't feel the same way about this town."

Monique returned with Luke's beer and set it down in front of him. Or almost in front of him. She was so busy staring out the window that she almost missed the table. Luke grabbed the beer just in time.

I did feel like Luke did about Verbena. Even if I hadn't wanted to move back, it had always been home. "Our little town has changed so much. Fast food. Marijuana growers. Eco-friendly car washes." I twisted again to see Professor Moonbeam get into his truck and drive away with it still unwashed. "Vandalism at the bank. Did you ever figure out who did that, Luke?"

He shook his head. "Nope. I must have looked at the security video a dozen times too."

I perked up. "There's video?"

"Yep. Even in Verbena, Big Brother is watching you," Jasmine said.

"Could I see it?" I asked.

Luke looked at me, his blue eyes narrowing down to a squint. "Why?"

"Don't you think you should have looked at it again?" I asked. "Someone writes 'Die, Banker. Die.' And then the banker dies? Doesn't that seem like something to check out?"

"Come by the station tomorrow, Death Ray. I'll show it to you. There's nothing to check out. You can't see who it is. Plus, I've already got the person who killed Alan in jail."

"No. You don't. I've told you that." I leaned forward to make my point.

"You've told me that, but you haven't given me any proof. I go by the evidence, not by how I feel about people." He moved forward too. He wasn't going to give an inch.

Sadly, he was right. I hadn't given him anything concrete. I needed to give him more than feelings. I shook my head. Mark came back with Jasmine's credit card. She signed the bill. "I'm going to go home and check on Donna and get out of these clothes." I gestured down at my heels and hose.

Luke choked on his beer. "See you 'round, Death Ray," he said as soon as he could breathe again.

I got up and straightened my shoulders. "Stop calling me that," I said.

"What?"

"Stop. Calling. Me. Death. Ray. Which of those words don't you understand?" I gripped the edge of the table.

He flushed. "I understood all the words. I didn't know you were so touchy about an old nickname."

I let go of the table. "Well, I am. So cut it out," I said.

He held his hands up in front of himself like a traffic cop. "Message received. No more Death Ray." His brow furrowed.

I hugged Jasmine and left. I went back to where I'd parked my car near the Civic Center. Half a block away, I could see the envelope tucked under the windshield wiper of the Element. A freaking parking ticket. I swear, Luke Butler waited around for me to park one inch over a line. It wasn't a ticket, though. It was a plain business envelope, the kind you buy by the hundreds at Costco. I opened it up and a photo slipped out.

I knew the photo. It was of Kyle and me when I was in eighth grade and had to build a catapult for my World History class. Dad was hopeless with tools, and Uncle Joey must have been busy. Kyle had stepped in. I'd dreaded working on it, but he'd made it so fun. The photo showed the two of us testing out the catapult. Our faces were next to each other's and so serious. I knew that minutes later, the two of us were laughing our butts off as the marshmallow we'd put in the catapult's cup had sailed yards farther than we'd imagined.

I couldn't count the times that Kyle had stepped in when Dad couldn't be there for Donna or for me for some reason or another. He'd driven carpools, attended meetings, brought forgotten lunches and sports equipment to school. He'd always been there when we needed him.

I thought about all the things I'd seen at Alan's funeral that day, from people taking photos of him in his casket to Marie spitting on his grave. And what about the vandal that wanted him to die? Someone else was responsible for what happened to Alan. Someone had set Kyle up for it. Kyle needed me to prove that, and I wasn't going to let him down. I'd lost one dad; I wasn't going to lose another.

I got in the car and blasted the air-conditioner, and then I called Lola. "Is there any way Marie Ruiz would have access to your house? Has she ever visited or anything?"

"Sure. She cuts my hair, and when I was laid up with that broken ankle last year, she would come out and give me a trim. Such a sweet girl." Then she paused. "Why?"

"Who else has been at your house in the past year?" I asked.

"Half the town when we were a stop on the garden tour."

"You had a garden tour at your house?"

"It wasn't just us. We were one stop on it. People mainly came to see the rose arbor. It's very popular."

I wasn't surprised. Donna and Greg had gotten married beneath it. The pictures looked like a spread from a magazine. "Who all goes on garden tours?"

There was a pause. "Pretty much anyone interested in gardening, Desiree."

"Just rose gardening?"

"Oh, no. All kinds of gardening."

Chapter Fifteen

After I got home and changed, I went into the living room and sat on the floor next to the couch where Donna was stretched out.

"What's up?" she asked, her fingers flying with her crochet hook.

"Will you teach me how to do one of those video things you do?" I asked. One of the things that Donna had added to the Turner Family Funeral Home menu was memorial videos. Family members could give her videos and photos and she would create a montage to be shown during either the viewing or the wake. The family could have it as a keepsake afterward. She was great at it. Me? Not so much. I was more of a word girl than a visual image girl.

"Why do you want to know?" she asked.

"So I can start making them." It seemed like a pretty obvious answer.

"Why would you need to do that? That's my job." I didn't think it was possible, but she actually started crocheting faster.

"Totally your job, but since you're not supposed to be doing your job right now, I thought it would be a good idea for you to show me." I nudged her with the laptop.

She didn't set down her yarn. "It would be more work to show you how to do it than to just do it myself."

I felt like this was one of those "teach a man to fish" moments. Yes, it would take longer in the short run to teach me, but it would save time and trouble in the future. I turned to make this argument to Donna but then saw something on her face.

It was a tear.

"Whoa, whoa, whoa! What's going on here?" She was not crying over memorial videos. Okay, she sometimes cried over memorial videos, but then it was over sweet images of fathers cuddling babies or of grandparents teaching a grandchild to fish, not about who got to do what (or who had to do what) around here.

She wiped at her cheek. "I don't know. I had this moment, you know? Like you were going to take over everything, and I'd lose the baby, and then I wouldn't have anything."

I got up on my knees and put my arms around her. "You're not going to lose the baby."

"You can't know that." She hiccupped against my shoulder.

Damn it, she was right. Don't make promises you can't keep. It was one of Dad's primary rules about how to conduct yourself. "Okay, how about this? There's no reason to assume you're going to lose the baby. You've got a great doctor who's being cautious and careful."

She grabbed my arm. "What if there's something wrong with me?" Her blue eyes looked huge in her face.

"There's nothing wrong with you." I paused, knowing how empty that promise was. I regrouped. "If there *is* something wrong, Dr. Chao will find it, and we'll figure it out from there."

"What if it's not a physical thing?" Her chin trembled.

I sat back down on the floor. "What kind of thing are you worried about?"

"What if I've been around death so much I can't make something live?" Her voice sounded clogged, as if she was trying not to cry.

I tried to work through what she was getting at. "Do you mean the chemicals and stuff downstairs? Do you think they caused some kind of permanent damage?"

She shook her head again. "No, not the chemicals. All the death. Mom died so young. Now Dad is gone too. We're around death all the time. What if there's something about being surrounded by death that makes a little life not want to continue?"

"You read all the funeral director information. Have you heard of anything that indicates women who work in the industry have more problems having babies than any other group?" A statistic like that would be the first thing I would look for as a reporter.

"No. I haven't, but maybe it's because nobody talks about it. Like it's one of those things that nobody wants to acknowledge." Her hand went to her belly.

I drew my legs up and rested my chin against my knees and thought for a moment. "First, I think if there was something like that, it wouldn't be a secret. People would talk. Second, Dad always said that he didn't think about what we did as being death-centered. He said it was about being part of the whole big circle of existence. Without death, there can't be new life."

She sighed. "That sounds a little *Lion King*."

"Do you want me to sing? Because I will if it'll help." I smiled, knowing what the answer would be.

She struggled into a sitting position. "No, that's quite all right. No singing necessary."

"And I don't want to take over everything. You know that." I had made that pretty damn clear in my teens.

"I don't know that anymore. I don't know what you want." There was snuffling, and I wondered if I was going to have to take another shower to wash snot out of my hair.

"Well, that's only because *I* don't know what I want. As soon as I figure it out, we'll both feel a whole lot better, right?" I thought for a moment. "How about we ask Dr. Chao if you can do work that lets you stay on the couch. You can put together the videos and make phone calls to suppliers. Then you can stop crocheting baby blankets at Olympic speeds and stop worrying about me taking your job." And I could stop screwing up orders and making crappy videos with bad editing. Win-win as far as I was concerned.

"Do you think she'll let me?" She blinked away tears.

"I think if you tell her your stress level is higher from not working than it was from working and that you're in danger of drowning in a sea of yarn, then I do think she'll let you." I paused for a second. "What about Greg?"

"What about him?"

"He's pretty worried about you. Will he be okay with this?" Honestly, Greg's stress level was nearly as concerning as Donna's. Lately, he had that wild-eyed look about him that horses get when they smell smoke.

"Let's do it first and tell him about it later. It's hard to argue with something when it's already done." She set down the blanket.

"Easier to ask forgiveness than permission." Another one of Dad's adages.

We fist-bumped and I handed her the computer. "I need a video for Ms. Stratton. Everything the family gave me is in a folder on the desktop."

"Got it." She took the computer from me like a man in a desert taking a glass of water, reverently but greedily. "Oh, thanks for the yarn, by the way."

I had not gotten Donna more yarn. It seemed too enabling. "I didn't get you any." A weird feeling slithered up my spine. "Where did you find it?"

"Greg found it." She looked up. "On the porch."

"The porch where he also found the baby crib charm?" I asked.

She nodded.

I pulled out the photo of Kyle and me and handed it to her. "This was on my car tonight. Something's not right."

"I agree it's weird, but so far it's been nice stuff, right?" She flipped open the computer.

"That doesn't make it any less creepy," I said. Maybe Jasmine wasn't the only one with a stalker.

"Mm-hmm," she replied, clearly already involved in her plans for Ms. Stratton's video. "Creepy."

I was about to leave when her head came up. "You got some packages, by the way. Uncle Joey put them in your room. There's a bunch of them. What is it?"

"Oh, just some things to freshen it up in there." I hurried to my room. My new drapes, comforter, and sheets had arrived. Suddenly I felt a lot perkier. I stripped the bed down and made it with the new linens. I took down the lace eyelet curtains with the pink ribbons and put up the floor-length drapes. Everything in soft shades of gray and sage green. Not a heart or a flower on anything.

I turned and looked around. Better. It was better. But now the old rag rug clashed with everything. I got on my laptop and started looking at area rugs.

There was always something new to work on, wasn't there? What was it that Janet had said to me? We're all a work in progress?

Chapter Sixteen

The Verbena Free Press

THURSDAY, JULY 18

Hearing Scheduled for Murder Suspect

A hearing will be held in the matter of the murder of Alan Brewer on July 18 at the Verbena Courthouse. Formal charges are being brought against Mr. Kyle Hansen of Verbena. Judge Gunderson will preside.

Mr. Hansen is being represented by Janet Provost. Ms. Provost again has claimed that Mr. Hansen is absolutely not guilty of the charges brought against him and feels that his name will be cleared and the charges will be dropped very soon.

The next morning after making sure that Donna didn't need anything, I went back to the police station. "I'm here to see Detective Butler," I told the cop at the desk.

He hadn't even finished dialing when Luke popped his head out. "This way, Death . . . I mean, Desiree."

I followed him back to a cubicle. He sat down at a computer monitor and started hitting buttons. A grainy image of the front of Verbena Union Bank popped up with a time and date stamp from April. In jerky motion, a figure wearing a hoodie pulled up over its head pulled out a can of spray paint and went to work.

"I have five more nearly identical segments of tape," he said, leaning back in his chair. "One from each time the bank was vandalized in the past year."

"What does it mean?" I asked, still trying to process the information.

"It means someone really didn't like Alan," he said. "It doesn't mean that whoever vandalized the bank killed him."

"Do you know who it was?" I couldn't tell anything from the video. It was too grainy, and the person was too covered up.

"Nope." He shook his head. "They keep their face turned away from the camera. There is one thing, though."

"What?"

He rewound to when the figure first walked into view. "Check out the shoes."

I leaned in to get a better look. High-top Chucks with a design. "What is it?" I asked.

"Hearts."

"So here you have someone painting death threats to Alan on the front door of his business, and you have Kyle locked up for killing him?" I sat back again in my chair.

"I didn't arrest Kyle on a whim, Desiree," he said. "It's where the evidence pointed."

"Then the evidence is wrong, Luke." I crossed my arms over my chest, feeling both frustrated and disappointed all at once. I wanted there to be an answer on that videotape. I wanted it to be Marie Ruiz so I could give Luke a suspect. I also wanted to cast Luke as the villain in all this. Make him the incompetent local law enforcement. He wasn't, though. He may have settled on Kyle as his suspect too quickly, but I could see how he got there. It was just like high school all over again. It was a mistake to discount him.

Another thought occurred to me. "Are there any other places with security cameras in town? Places that would give you access to the tape?"

"Like where?" he asked.

I bit my lip. "Like the Civic Center."

"Why?" he asked.

"Someone left something on my car. I wanted to see who it might be." Maybe there'd be some videotape and I could find out who was leaving little things on my car.

"What kind of something?" His eyes narrowed. "Something nasty? Do you need to make a report?"

"Just a photo. I wondered who had left it, though." His sudden serious tone made me smile.

He tapped on the keyboard and peered at the computer screen. "They have a camera, but it's only one angle, and they don't keep the tape long. When would it have been?"

"Last night while I was at Tappiano's with you."

His mouth made a little *O*. He tapped at the keyboard again and an image of the Civic Center came up. You couldn't see my car from the angle of the camera, but you could see the parking lot. Luke rewound until the time was for just a bit before I would have left the reception. We watched as various people, some more recognizable than others, left the building and walked into the parking lot. Then something caught my eye. "Wait," I said. "Go back."

He rewound a little.

"Now stop." In the upper corner of the image I could see some legs walking through the parking lot. Long legs. The person was tall. I squinted at the feet. Deck shoes. Half the men in the area wore those. Dad had had at least three pairs. Whoever it was hadn't come from the Civic Center but from somewhere behind the building, and it had been at a moment when no one else was coming or going.

"Just legs and shoes, again," Luke said. "And there's no guarantee they're going to your car. Here's when you left," he said, fast-forwarding.

I saw my legs and Jasmine's legs as we went to our cars. I wouldn't have known it was us if I hadn't known what shoes we were wearing. I sat back, even more disappointed than I'd been before, but this time with an idea on how to go forward. Then another pair of legs walked past in the exact same direction that we had gone. "Who's that?"

Luke shrugged. "How should I know? Whoever it was came after you left. They couldn't have left anything on your car."

He had a point. It still made me uneasy somehow, but then a squad car pulled through the parking lot. "Look," Luke said. "It's Officer Haynes. It's all good."

It didn't feel all good, but I couldn't say precisely why.

*   *   *

There were no bodies to pick up, no remains to be delivered, no visitations to schedule, no viewings to coordinate, and Kyle's hearing wasn't for a few hours. It happened that way sometimes. There'd be days we were slammed with two or three events going on in the same day and then stretches of time where nobody in the area seemed to be dying and needing our services.

It had been hard on Dad not to be able to be predictable. He never knew when he'd be needed.

Those quiet periods of time—like now—were great times to schedule dentist appointments, eye checks, and haircuts. It was also a great time to see if I could drum up some proof that Marie Ruiz might have had something to do with Alan's murder. She knew her way around Kyle and Lola's house. The gun cabinet wasn't hidden. She would have seen it when she'd been there to trim Lola's hair so she had the means. Figuring out her motive was my next step. She hated him, but why? I phoned Marie, who happened to have an opening. I checked in with Donna and then walked over to the Cut 'n' Curl.

I slid into the chair, and Marie snapped the purple apron around my neck. "So what are we going to do today?" She fluffed through my hair.

"I'm not sure. I definitely need at least a trim. I'd like something easy." I'd like to never look at another flat iron in my life.

Marie cocked her head to one side as she lifted my hair off my shoulders. "How short do you want to go?"

I shrugged. I wasn't sure I cared. "Whatever you think."

"You know, with some layers, you'd really release some of the natural wave." She gave me a sly smile as if she was suggesting I do something illicit. "You could keep the length then."

Natural wave. It sounded appealing. "Sounds great."

She tilted me back so my head was in the sink and started washing my hair. "I'm so sorry about your dad." She worked shampoo through my hair.

I braced. Dad was still a hard topic for me to talk about. "Thanks."

She rinsed away the shampoo with warm water and started on the conditioner. "He was a good guy. I used to sit next to him at some of the VDBA meetings. He was such a great presence in the room. So kind. So reasonable. The whole town misses him."

I swallowed hard. I probably wouldn't be the first person to cry while getting their hair washed at the salon, but it wasn't really a club I wanted to join.

"I still can't believe he's gone. I always thought he'd show back up," she said.

"Me too." It was true. There was a part of me that still thought he was going to show up. I'd turn around and there he'd be, with that slightly crooked smile, his hair maybe a little longer than it should be. He'd muss my hair, a habit that made me insane from the time I was seven until now, when I would give anything to experience it again. He'd explain how he was swept out onto an island where he survived on berries until he could figure out how to get back to shore or had amnesia and had been working as a short-order cook in a small town or was adopted by a school of dolphins. Then my world would be right again. Because it was definitely not right now. Not even close.

"He had such a great aura. You could see it glowing from across a room."

I didn't think I'd ever seen my dad's aura. It was good to know that someone had and thought it looked good. As much as I wanted to pursue the subject, I knew that I had a good segue into the topic I really needed to know about and decided to take it. "I guess you didn't feel the same about Alan Brewer's aura."

She stopped massaging my scalp for a second. "How did you know that?"

I looked up again, wondering now how wise it was to bring these things up when I was in such a vulnerable position. "I saw you say good-bye to him at the cemetery."

"Oh," she said. "I didn't see you."

"I was standing in the shade over near the edge of the cemetery," I said. "It probably looked like everyone was gone."

"Yeah, I'm not sure I would have spit on him like that if I'd known anyone was watching, even though he deserved it completely." She went back to massaging my scalp. She made a noise in the back of her throat like she might have to spit. My eyes opened in alarm. I didn't want her to hock a loogie in my hair. "Though maybe I would have. That son of a bitch can rot in hell for all I care. His aura was a murky, nasty mess."

"What did he do that was so bad?" I asked.

She hesitated, then brought me back to a sitting position and wrapped a towel around my wet hair. "I'd own this shop right now if it wasn't for Alan Brewer."

"How so?" This was getting good.

She sighed. "Two years ago, Vanessa, the owner here, wanted to retire. Her feet are bad. Her back is bad. She was ready to rest. She wanted to sell it to me, but I didn't have the cash. I went to the bank to see if I could get a small business loan."

It didn't take an aura reader to see where this was going. "Alan wouldn't give you the loan?"

She led me over to the chair in front of the mirror. "Oh, he would have given it to me all right. He would have given it to me big time. In fact, I think he meant to give it to me right there on the desk. It was what I would have had to give in return that was the problem."

I sat down and became very still. "You don't mean . . ."

"Oh, I so do mean. You know he even drew the blinds in his office? Like I'd do it right there in the bank. With half the town outside cashing checks and making deposits." She removed the towel and combed through my hair.

"You're kidding." Thinking of Alan as a cheater wasn't much of a stretch. After all, he'd cheated on Christine with Rosemarie. But shaking down people in the community for sexual favors? Right there in the bank? That reached a level of ick I hadn't anticipated. No wonder Johanna looked a little nauseated as she'd sat at his desk. I hoped she'd sterilized it first.

"Nope. Not kidding. Not one little bit." She paused. "Here's the thing that really gets me. He did it all like he expected it to work. Which tells me that it's probably worked before. I wonder how many women have had to get down on their knees in that office to get a loan."

I thought about all the other honey blondes at the funeral who had opened new businesses in the past year. Trixie Warner, Ella Keller, and Mandy Smith all had opened brand-new businesses. I'd be willing to bet all of them had some pretty interesting terms on their loans. Would that give them motive? Probably not. I drummed my heels against the salon chair in frustration. They'd probably want to keep him alive so nobody would look too closely into those loans.

The bell over the door tinkled, signaling an incoming customer. "Hold on a sec," Marie said and stepped around to the front. "Can I help you?"

"Yeah," a voice said. "Remember that serum you were telling me about the last time I was in? The one that would protect my hair from the flat iron?"

"Sure. It's right here. Did you decide to buy it?" Marie asked.

"Yeah. I tried the drugstore ones, but they're not as good, you know?" The voice sounded familiar, but I couldn't quite place it.

"I do. I know it's expensive, but you don't use as much and it works so well. It's really worth it. I mean, it's your hair, right? It's like the first thing that everyone sees."

"Totally. How much?"

"Forty-two."

"Here you go. Oh, and do you have time for a mani-pedi?"

"I've got someone in my chair right now. Come back in an hour?"

"Great."

"See you then, Monique."

Marie returned to me. "So what are we going to do today?" she asked as she sat me up.

"I'm thinking the layers sound good," I said.

"You got it. I think you're going to love it. Those beachy waves are totally in right now. You should absolutely take advantage of it."

So Marie Ruiz had a good reason to hate Alan, and she had a bit of angry streak based on being willing to spit on someone's grave. There was her motive. She'd been in Lola and Kyle's house and knew where the gun was kept and probably knew Kyle's clockwork schedule. There was means. Now, what about opportunity?

"So where were you when you heard about Alan being shot?" I asked. "I figure it's kind of like our generation of Verbenaites knowing where they were when they heard Kennedy was shot."

Marie frowned and thought for a moment, scissors momentarily paused above my head. I watched her eyes in the mirror. "You know, I think I was just finishing up over at the senior center. Or maybe it was when I was going home from the grocery store." She shrugged and started snipping again. "Either way, I was in my car. You?"

"When he was brought into the funeral home. What do you do at the senior center?" Maybe it would be something I could check on. See if she truly had an alibi.

"This." She gestured at herself and the scissors. "It's hard for a lot of them to get to a salon so I go there once a week. Say, if you ever need help with people's hair at Turner, you let me know, okay?"

She finished the cut, blew out my hair, and then handed me the mirror. "Wow," I said. "I didn't even know my hair would do that!"

"It just needed to be cut in a way that releases the curl. You don't even have to blow-dry it if you don't want to. You can towel-dry it, rub in a little product, and go." She twirled me around so I could see the back.

I almost gasped. "You are a true artist."

She giggled. "I've always understood hair. It's like it speaks to me."

I was really starting to hope that Marie Ruiz had nothing to do with Alan's death. This was seriously the best haircut I'd had in years. Maybe ever. Maybe I could visit her in prison and she could cut my hair. They probably frowned on people bringing in scissors for inmates, though.

Chapter Seventeen

Kyle's arraignment was set for three PM. I got there
a little early to make sure I had a good seat and to
watch the crowd. For years, Pluma Vista had used the
same beautiful art deco courthouse, but it had the same
problems the police station did. Too much twenty-first-
century technology to cram into a twentieth-century
building. Two years ago, they'd opened the new courthouse. Outside, it was all glass and chrome. Inside, it
was all fresh paint and carpeting just above industrial
grade. The courtrooms were smaller than the old ones
but better set up for modern trials, with AV outlets and
computer hookups and all the bells and whistles anyone would want. There were three long benches for
lookers-on. I took a spot near the end of the second row.
At two forty-five, the assistant district attorney for Pluma
Vista County, Tommy Lomax, strode in and took his
place behind the desk on the right.

He was exactly what I expected an assistant district attorney to be. White, young, male. A little soft in the middle from too many takeout lunches eaten at his desk. A very tiny bald spot that he might not even know about yet forming on the top of his head.

Then Janet arrived. She had on a pantsuit with low heels and was wheeling a milk-crate-on-wheels kind of thing behind her. She saw me as she made her way to her table at the front of the courtroom. "Desiree, good. You're here. That's a lovely color on you," she said, gesturing to my top. "And your hair looks amazing."

"Uh, thanks. Do you need any help?" I asked, gesturing at her box.

She waved me away. "Oh, no. I've got this. Is Lola coming?"

I nodded. "She should be here in a few minutes."

"Move into the front row, dear, and save her a spot, okay?" She patted my arm.

I got up and moved, placing my purse next to me to take up space. The benches began to fill up. A murder in Pluma Vista County was big news. But a murder over a neighborhood dispute? It was the stuff that people who wrote hooks for television news broadcasts dreamed of. Is your neighbor plotting to kill you? How far would your neighbor go? Danger at home. Unsafe in the house. I knew I would have had a field day with it if I'd still been a working journalist and I didn't know the people involved. I felt a little nudge of guilt. I'd had a field day with cases like these. I'd rarely given a second thought to what the people involved were actually going through.

"Nice haircut." Rafe slid into the seat next to me. "Hey, Desiree. Anything to say before the hearing begins?"

"No comment." I pushed my purse farther. "I'm saving this spot for someone."

"I don't see a reserved sign." He flashed that big, bright smile at me.

"Move," I said and turned back to face the front.

"And if I say no?" he asked.

"Want to see what happens if I tell the bailiff you're bothering me?" I asked.

We both looked over at the bailiff, who was about seventy years old and stood like he might have a bum knee. "I think I could take him."

I started to rise, and he grabbed my arm and pulled me back down.

"Okay, okay. I'm moving."

Luckily, Lola showed up a few minutes later. She slid in next to me. "Thanks," she whispered.

I took her hand. It shook a little.

Then they led in Kyle. Cuffed at the wrists and ankles, he shuffled to the table where Janet sat, file folders spread out before her. I was glad they'd let him change into street clothes. There were a few people outside dressed like zebras in black-and-white-striped jumpsuits. They looked like escapees from an old-timey cartoon about convicts. It couldn't make a good impression if you had to go in front of a judge dressed like that.

Lola gasped when she saw him and started to stand. The bailiff took one wonky step toward us, and I pulled Lola down beside me just like Rafe had done to me. "Stay cool," I said.

"I'm trying." She slipped a tissue out of her bag and dabbed at her eyes.

Kyle sat down at the table, and they uncuffed him. He turned to see Lola and gave her a little wave, which started a fresh round of shaking from her. Then the bailiff was doing the "Hear ye, hear ye" thing, and we all stood for the judge, who waved at us all to sit.

The bailiff read out the case number, and the judge looked over the files in front of him. "Ms. Provost, how does your client plead?"

Janet stood. "My client pleads not guilty, Your Honor. In fact, I think you'll find in front of you a brief asking for the charges to be dismissed."

ADA Lomax rolled his eyes. "Seriously? On what grounds?"

"On the grounds that you have no evidence connecting my client to the murder, and do not take that tone with me, young man." Janet shook a finger at him. "I know your mother."

ADA Lomax turned very red. "Excuse me?"

"Yes. I used to play mah-jongg with her on Thursday nights. I know how proud she is of you and how much she'd hate to hear that you'd been disrespectful," Janet said.

The judge tapped his gavel. "That's enough, you two. Mr. Lomax, do you have anything?"

Lomax glanced down at the legal pad in front of him. "We have the gun that was used to kill Mr. Brewer. The gun belonged to Mr. Hansen."

"A gun that could have been stolen from the home anytime in the two weeks before the murder," Janet chimed in. "It's a gun, but it's hardly smoking."

Judge Gunderson bit back a smile. "Yet it does seem to tie your client to the incident enough to warrant going forward with the trial."

"If you say so," Janet said. She paused, head cocked to one side. "May I approach the bench, Judge Gunderson?"

"Of course." He beckoned to her. Lomax started toward the bench too. Janet turned to him. "This doesn't concern you."

"Excuse me, but if you're saying something to the judge, then I get to hear it." He crossed his arms over his chest.

She rolled her eyes. "Fine, but I'm telling you it has nothing to do with you."

"I'll be the judge of that," he snapped.

Janet went the rest of the way to the bench and whispered something very quietly.

The judge's hand flew to his face. "Did I get it?" he asked, his voice low.

"A little lower," Janet said.

He moved his hand lower and wiped away what had been a nearly invisible smudge. "Thank you. I wonder how many people saw that there and let me walk around like that."

Janet shrugged. "There are all kinds of friends in the world." She tossed a look at Lomax and returned to our table.

"Shall we discuss bail?" Judge Gunderson asked.

Lomax stayed standing. "The people ask for one million dollars in bail."

Janet made a noise in the back of her throat like she might need to spit. "That's ridiculous, Your Honor. Mr. Hansen is an upstanding member of our community with no record. His wife is a teacher, and he runs a consulting business from their home. They hardly have the wherewithal to make that kind of bail."

Lomax turned to her. "Does he have a passport?"

"I don't know," she snapped back. "What difference would that make?"

"This is a first-degree murder charge. He wouldn't be the first person accused of a crime of this magnitude to make a run for it." Lomax rested one hip against his table. He clearly felt like he was getting the best of this argument.

Janet threw her hands in the air. "So take his passport, if he even has one. He's not going anywhere. He's staying right here and clearing his name. In case you forgot, we pled not guilty. We meant not guilty."

Lomax turned to Judge Gunderson. "Judge, this is grandstanding, pure and simple."

Janet clutched her hand to her chest. "I'm grandstanding? I'm not the one asking a self-employed man with property and ties in the area to cough up a million dollars so he doesn't flee from a charge of which he is entirely and completely innocent."

The judge banged his gavel. "Enough, you two. Save the theatrics for the trial." He rubbed at the spot where the smudge had been. "Bail is set at two thousand dollars." He banged his gavel and stood. Everyone in the courtroom leapt to their feet.

As he left, Janet waved. "Bye, Judge Gunderson. Say hello to your grandmother for me. Tell her we miss her at water aerobics."

He ducked his head. "I will, Ms. Provost."

Lomax rolled his eyes and shook his finger at Janet. "You can play the sweet mom in the courtroom all you want, Ms. Provost. I've heard about you and what you do. You will not be getting away with it on my watch."

"I'm sorry you feel so threatened, Tommy. You're a very smart boy. I think you're going to be fine." She reached into her briefcase and pulled out a plate covered with plastic wrap. "Cookie?"

We all stood around clapping Kyle on the back and congratulating Janet on a job well done and eating snicker-doodles. We were so focused on our relief that no one even noticed Rosemarie until she was right up on top of us. She vibrated with pent-up energy. "I will be watching you, Kyle Hansen!" She raised one finger and pointed it at him in a classic *j'accuse* pose. "Don't think I won't be!"

I heard cameras clicking all around us. The tableau was going to look awfully good on some front pages.

Lola stepped between Rosemarie and Kyle. "Watch all you want, Rosemarie. Kyle is innocent. He didn't do anything wrong, and he won't do anything wrong."

"He better not! I'll have the police out there to arrest him again so fast, his head will spin!" Rosemarie screamed.

Lola waved a hand at her as if to dismiss her and then turned. It was probably a bad choice. Rosemarie couldn't seem to resist and grabbed a hank of Lola's hair, yanking hard. Lola screamed, and I thought we were about to have an instant replay of the fistfight from Delia Burns's funeral, but the bailiff acted surprisingly quickly considering that bum knee. He had Rosemarie by the waist in a matter of seconds. He practically carried her from the courtroom.

Lola rubbed at her head. "I'm getting really tired of her pulling my hair."

Janet patted her arm. "We'll consider a civil suit about it once we prove Kyle's innocence."

*   *   *

Lola and Kyle had invited me back to their place to celebrate their victory, but I thought they deserved some time alone. Plus, I had something I wanted to check out. Before we all parted ways, I took Kyle aside.

"You'd tell me if my dad had had some kind of secret, wouldn't you?" I asked.

"What kind of secret?" He rubbed at his wrists as if they still were cuffed.

"I'm not sure, but I found this in his desk." I held up the key. "And the desk was less dusty than the rest of the room. It looked like someone else might have been looking for something in it."

He took it from me and examined it. "It's just a key, Desiree."

"To a storage space, I think. A storage space that I don't think he needed. What if . . ." I hesitated to say what I was thinking. "What if Dad isn't really dead?"

Kyle's eyes opened wide. "If your father was alive, he'd be here with you and Donna. You found a key and now you think he's not dead? That's a huge leap, Desiree."

"No." I shook my head. "It's not. There are other things too." I told him about the charms and the yarn and the photo. "I'm going to check it out anyway."

He thought for a second, rubbing his chin. "I think that's a good idea. Then you won't have to wonder. There'll be some easy explanation for all of it." He pulled me into a hug. He smelled like soap and toothpaste just like Dad used to. He felt like home. Something caught in my throat—and was there something in my eye too? Damn it. Stupid allergies. "Don't get your hopes up, okay? I'd hate to watch you go through mourning your father all over again. I know it was hard on you not to have found his body, but still alive? Why would he do something like that?"

I sighed. "I kind of hoped you would know."

We all said good-bye. It made my heart glad to watch Lola and Kyle walking out of the courthouse hand in hand.

I'd already looked up where Pluma Vista Storage was. It wasn't far. I made it there in about thirty minutes. I pulled up to the gate. There was a box to punch numbers into. What would Dad use as his code? I knew what he always used to use, so I tried that first. My birthday and then Donna's birthday. Presto! The gate slid open.

I drove in until I found the right block of spaces and then got out of the car. The sun glaring off the cement blinded me for a second. Once I adjusted, I went up the stairs and found the space whose number corresponded to the one on the key ring. The key turned easily in the lock. I slid the metal latch aside and lifted the door.

It was a small space—maybe five feet by five feet—and there wasn't much in it. Mainly a few boxes. I opened the first one. Photo albums. Probably five of them. I flipped one of them open. Pictures of Donna. Pictures of me. Pictures of Mom. I picked up another one. Same thing.

I moved that box aside and opened the one beneath it. Some papers and a smaller box, no bigger than a large kitchen match box. I opened the smaller box. It was full of charms.

I went through the rest of the boxes. It was definitely Dad's stuff. There was no denying that. I still didn't know why he felt he needed to keep it here. I closed everything back up and made my way to the office. A big guy with a backward baseball hat sat behind the desk.

"Hi," I said. "I'd like to ask about a storage space."

"Right on," he said. "We got lots of those. How big did you need?"

"I think I might already have one. Sort of." I fingered the key in my pocket.

"So what is it you need?" He looked confused. I didn't blame him.

I decided to lay it out for him. I told him about my dad and then finding the key.

"And you want me to do what?" he asked, again scratching at his forehead.

"I was hoping you could tell me who is paying the rent on that space. My sister and I aren't." I bit my lip.

"Not sure I can tell you that." He shook his head. "Privacy issues and all that."

"Is anyone paying for it?" I asked. "Could you tell me that much?"

He squinted as he thought. "I maybe could do that. What was the number again?"

I told him, and he turned to his computer. After a few seconds of tapping, he said, "That unit was rented eighteen months ago. The rent on it was prepaid for two years."

Eighteen months. That was two months before Dad disappeared. "Thanks," I said.

I got back in my car with no more answers than I'd had going in. Why had Dad needed that space? What was going on eighteen months ago? Nothing really. I was still working at the television station and loving it. Donna had just found out she was pregnant. Everything was good.

Or did I only think it was good?

Chapter Eighteen

The Verbena Free Press

FRIDAY, JULY 19

Widow Breaks Down at Bail Hearing

Upon hearing that her husband's alleged murderer was to be released on bail to return to his home directly next to hers, Rosemarie Brewer was shocked—so shocked that she confronted Mr. Hansen, his wife, and his attorney, promising that she would be watching them carefully and would summon the police at the slightest indication of danger to herself or her property.

According to Ms. Brewer, Ms. Hansen made a threatening gesture toward her. She felt she had no recourse but to defend herself: "The system was doing nothing to protect me. I had no one to turn to but myself. So I took matters into my own hands."

No other witnesses saw the threatening gesture.

Along with matters, Ms. Brewer took a large hunk of Ms. Hansen's hair, which she used to pull Ms. Hansen toward the floor. At that point, Bailiff Falk heard the fracas and intervened. "I don't know what started it," Falk said. "I just know that Rosemarie was spitting mad. I thought I was going to have to call for backup to get her out of there."

Janet Provost, attorney for Mr. and Ms. Hansen, said, "I understand Ms. Brewer's frustration. I, too, wish the authorities would find the person responsible for her husband's murder and put that person behind bars. That person, however, is not my client. While we have great sympathy for Ms. Brewer and her loss, we cannot allow her to attack innocent people. If she continues to do so, there will be repercussions."

Madeline Ledbetter was pulling out all the funeral stops for her mother. We were having the trifecta of events (viewing, graveside service, wake). She'd chosen the Empire casket. Not exactly the Michael Jackson of caskets, but it was no plain pine box either. There was a memory box, a design on the interior, and a heavy-duty gasket to ward off the effects of moisture and soil for as long as possible. She'd selected several casket accessories that reflected her mother's interests and causes: trinkets with an embroidery hoop, a garden trowel, and a bingo card. All that was draped with a lovely casket blanket. There was a program, a video, and a playlist. I'd drawn the line at funeral doves. She'd been a little disappointed, but it was one thing we just didn't do at Turner, and I didn't want to start.

Uncle Joey had wheeled Mrs. Ledbetter in and placed her at the front of the Magnolia Room. I had the music that Madeline had chosen playing over the sound system. Olive, Henrietta, and Grace did not approve.

"What the hell is that?" Olive asked me as I seated them and gathered their walkers.

"Native American flute music. Apparently, Ms. Stratton found it soothing in the last days of her life." I hefted the three walkers up.

"She was deaf as a doornail. Probably couldn't even hear it over all those machines they had going, keeping her alive," Henrietta chimed in.

Madeline had done pretty much everything there was to do and more to keep her mother alive. I looked over to where she was sitting, handkerchief to her face to catch the tears that streamed down her cheeks. Poor thing.

"Should have let her go three weeks ago," Grace said. "I, for one, don't buy it."

"Buy what?" I wasn't aware that anyone was selling anything.

She gestured at Madeline. "All the tears. All the wailing. All the heroic efforts. All the gewgaws. It's nothing but posturing."

I looked over at Madeline. "She's really distraught, Grace. I don't think I've seen her stop crying since her first call to us."

Henrietta shook her head. "She should have put a little more effort in when Virginia was alive and could appreciate it. Grace is right. This is a classic case of over-compensation. She was a rotten teenager, you know."

I didn't know, nor did I think Uncle Joey would approve of me gossiping about our client during the service. "I need to go check on the guest book," I said.

"Oh! Remember the time Maddie stole Virginia's car and drove to Vegas with her girlfriends?" Olive asked.

I stopped and looked back over at Madeline, with her tasteful black dress, sensible shoes, and discreet purse. "She stole a car?"

"Oh, yes. Wasn't she the one who mooned the whole town during the Fire Festival parade?" Grace asked.

Henrietta laughed. "Oh, yes. That was quite the show. She jumped onto the back of the fire truck while it was moving slow, dropped her trousers, and waggled her fanny at us."

"It was a miracle that Virginia didn't die right then of embarrassment." Grace gestured to Maddie again. "This? This is just a show so everyone will see that she's mourning appropriately. Notice how she's jamming it all into one day. Viewing, service, wake. Bam, bam, bam. Not going to spend any more time on it than she has to."

"What about all the trinkets and such? Those things cost money," Henrietta said.

"Overkill," Grace said with certainty. "Over-the-top overkill."

"Or maybe she feels really bad about how she treated her mother and is trying to get some closure but still has a job and things to tend to," I suggested.

Grace made a disgusted noise in the back of her throat. "You are your father's daughter, aren't you? Always trying to see the best in everyone." She said it as if it was a flaw I should be trying to overcome.

"Thank you," I said and stowed their walkers against the back wall, feeling somehow taller than I had a few minutes before. I floated out to the lobby area to make sure the guest book was in place. It was.

My phone buzzed. A text from Rafe: "Any comment on yesterday's hearing?"

I texted back an emoji of a face with a closed zipper where its mouth should be.

Everything went as it was supposed to. Pastor Campbell spoke and said some lovely words about Virginia. Her grandson read a poem that she liked that she had shared with him. Then it was time to say good-bye and go to the cemetery.

That's when everything went wrong.

I went up to the front to close the casket, signaling to the pallbearers that it was time to bear the casket out to the hearse, where Uncle Joey was waiting. Madeline leapt from her seat, screaming, "Mama, no! Mama, don't leave me!" and tried to leap into the casket before I could close it.

I screamed "No!" too and tried to keep the casket from tumbling over with Madeline's weight overbalancing it. One of the pallbearers tried to pull Madeline out. She bit him, and he reared back, effectively head-butting me in the nose.

I don't really know firsthand what happened after that. The next thing I knew, I was looking up to find Olive leaning over me. "Are you okay, dear?" she asked and handed me an ice pack.

I was on the floor, a trickle of blood running down from my nose. I sat up slowly, touching my face to see if anything was broken. "What happened?"

"Your uncle came in and lifted Maddie out of the casket. He got the casket out to the hearse." She reached into the pouch hanging off the side of her walker and pulled out a tissue that she handed to me. "Such a fine, strong man, your uncle." Her tone was a little dreamy.

I held it to my nose. "Madeline? Where is she?"

"On her way to the cemetery too. All calmed down now." Olive pressed her lips together. "Overkill."

"Or great grief."

"Or great guilt. Sometimes they look pretty much the same."

Once everyone left, I took the opportunity to go lie down in my room for a bit with an ice pack on my nose. The empty walls mocked me. Maybe I should have put the girl on the rock and the kitten in the tree back up. No. That wasn't the right choice. Change is hard. Transitions suck. I just needed to get through this one, and the only way to do that was to go forward, not backward.

My other orders had arrived too: a plush area rug and a motion-sensitive security camera. I rolled up the rag rug, laid the new one on the floor, and then opened the box for the camera and read the instructions. I'd install it after this darn headache went away.

I looked around the room. It really was getting there. The rug and the drapes and the linens all looked great. The walls looked awfully bare now, though.

I settled into my bed with my icepack and a happy sigh.

*   *   *

When I walked into Tappiano's for Hometown Happy Hour that evening, Jasmine gave me the slow clap. "Nice," she said. "That might be the best haircut you've had ever."

"I was thinking the same thing." I fluffed it for her.

"The shiner, however? That is not quite so adorable." She took me by the chin and tilted my head for a better look.

"I tried to keep Madeline Ledbetter from climbing into the casket with her mother." I sat down next to her.

"You should have called your uncle," Jasmine said. She settled herself back on her high stool.

"I know that now." I settled myself in too and looked around. There were fewer whispers each time I walked in. That was good. Being the object of gossip was never fun. The room hummed with talk, and across the street the polo-shirted guys at the Clean Green Car Wash lounged in the shade. My world.

Monique came over with a carafe and a glass. "Care to sample the serrano sangria tonight? Mark's giving it a trial run before the Fire Festival."

"Sounds perfect."

She poured me a glass. Someone called her name from another table, and she gave us a little wave and left.

"So you went to Marie Ruiz?" Jasmine leaned in. "Did you learn anything?"

"Plenty." I leaned forward too. I explained about Alan and the terms of the loan he'd offered Marie and that she would have known where Kyle and Lola's gun was and how to get it.

"So what now?" Jasmine asked, her eyes wide.

"Now I check her alibi. She said she was at the senior center." I needed to be able to check her alibi without it looking like I was. I took a sip of the serrano sangria and spluttered. "I'm not sure I like my drinks to be spicy."

"You'll get used to it after another couple of sips. You asked her for an alibi?" Jasmine sat up straighter. "Just like that?"

"I was more subtle than that, but I got what I needed," I said feeling fairly satisfied. "Another couple of sips and all my taste buds will be burned."

Luke plopped down at the table. "Whoa, Death Ray. What does the other guy look like? Sorry, I mean Desiree."

He gave me an innocent look, but I had a suspicion he was trying to have his cake and eat it too. He still got to call me Death Ray, but I couldn't get mad about it. Or could I? "Don't be a jerk, Luke. I mean, I know it's your default position, but try to fight it, okay?"

He put his hands up in front of him. "Whoa! What's with all the aggro?"

"Anger can be really positive if expressed correctly. I tell my anger management group that all the time," Jasmine said and smiled at me.

"Fine, but I'm not in the group. Don't shrink me," I said.

"Or me," Luke chimed in.

She laughed. "Oh, you are way too easy to read to be fun to shrink, Luke."

He scowled. "I'm going to another table."

I clutched my chest. "Oh, woe is me!"

He glared but was true to his word and went off to talk to Bernadette Kim.

Jasmine watched him go and then asked, "What are you doing for the Fire Festival?"

"Ringtoss." I nodded. It's what we always did. Turner Family Funeral Home Ringtoss was a time-honored tradition at the Fire Festival. It was easy to set up, easy to tear down, easy to see if someone had actually won or not. One year, Vernell Trotter had set up a similar booth where you tossed rings over cones instead of posts. No one spoke to him for months. Our ringtoss was sacred.

Jasmine rolled her eyes. "Again? You always do a ring-toss. Can't you come up with something more interesting?" She had no respect for tradition.

"Like what?" I asked.

"I don't know. A fortune-teller, maybe?" she suggested.

I shot her a look. "We're a funeral home. As far as we're concerned, everyone's future is the same, and it's not anything anyone wants to hear at a festival. It's definitely not something you want to tell little kids unless you want to send the entire elementary school spinning into a depression."

"Good point, although it might not be bad for my business." She thought for a second. "What about roulette?"

"Brings to mind the Russian variety, don't you think?" It wasn't as if I hadn't thought about these possibilities.

She made a face. "Another good point."

"The ringtoss is fine. All the kids love the ringtoss." I nodded again.

She laughed. "That's because you give them prizes even if they don't win."

"And?" I didn't see a problem with that.

She pointed at me. "You're setting them up for unrealistic expectations in life."

"I'll let someone else burst their bubbles, thank you very much." It's not like the world didn't stand in line to do that anyway.

She cocked her head to one side so I knew a question was coming. "How come you didn't tell Luke about Marie Ruiz? He'd be able to check her alibi a lot more easily than you could."

I stared at her. "First, he's not interested in looking at anyone but Kyle. Second, do you not see this haircut? You know Luke would either tell her who had pointed him in her direction or she'd figure it out. I can't risk that."

Jasmine clinked her glass against mine. "Good to know your priorities are in place."

Chapter Nineteen

Fracas at Funeral Home

Overcome with grief at her mother's passing, Madeline Ledbetter crawled into the coffin and refused to get out. Several people attempted to remove her, including Desiree Turner, assistant funeral director at Turner Family Funeral Home. According to witnesses, Ms. Ledbetter fought all of them off. Pallbearers suffered a variety of bite wounds and bruises. Ms. Ledbetter was finally physically lifted out of the coffin by Joseph Turner. Order was restored, and the service continued as planned, but without Ms. Turner, who briefly lost consciousness.

Corrections

The *Verbena Free Press* printed an announcement of an information meeting on reverse mortgages being held at the Civic Center Danube Room. The *Free Press* mistakenly listed the person holding the meeting as Alan Brewer. The

meeting will be held by Johanna Powell, Mr. Brewer's asso-
ciate. The *Free Press* apologizes for the error and thanks the
readers who pointed out that Mr. Brewer is now deceased
and not likely to be present at the meeting.

*   *   *

Donna looked up from her computer when I walked
in with a cup of hot tea for her. "So Rafe Valdez is
still obsessed with you?" she asked.

"What?" I set down the tea.

She turned the computer to show me the *Verbena Free
Press* website. "There you are again."

"You read the *Free Press* online?" I asked. Apparently
my slipping the paper into the recycling before she could
see it had been for naught.

"You don't think I read the paper version, do you?
Joey's the one who always wants that." She turned the
computer back around. "Why?"

"Never mind." I was not anywhere near as slick as I
thought I was.

"What do you have on deck for today?" she asked.

"I thought I'd drop off some brochures at the senior
center." No one really thinks about marketing funeral
homes. Well, that's not true. Funeral directors do. It's a
delicate thing, though. It's not like a dress shop, where
you can run a sale or offer a BOGO special. Coupons
seemed pretty tacky too.

Turner Family Funeral Home made sure we were always a community presence. We'd have a booth at the Fire Festival. We'd contribute a prize for the Labor Day Fun Run. We'd give away poinsettias at the annual holiday craft fair. We sponsored a weekly movie at the Verbena Senior Center. It alternated between something recent and something classic. This week we were showing one of my personal favorites, *North by Northwest*. We'd get a good turnout for that one. While they were there, if people happened to pick up brochures about our planning services and the advantages to prepaying to be sure they'd get what they wanted when it was their turn, well, so be it.

That, of course, meant that I needed to make sure that there was a stock of brochures available to be picked up. I was always surprised at how many we ran through. It would also give me a chance to find out exactly what times Marie had been cutting hair on the morning that Alan was murdered.

"Hey, welcome back!" Arleen said from behind the front desk when I walked in.

I smiled. "Thanks. Just dropping off some brochures to have around during the movie."

"I'm glad you brought them by. We're almost out. Do you still have any of those little sticky notes? Those are in high demand too. People stick them to their belongings so the kids will know who's supposed to get what."

A Grave Issue

"I'll drop some by next week." I peeked into the big meeting room. It was full of people. "What's going on in there?"

"Tai chi. Very popular. It's supposed to help with your balance. Nobody wants to fall and break a hip." Arleen peeked in too.

"True enough." I arranged the brochures on the table under the bulletin board, scanning the notices by force of habit. Dog sitting. Piano lessons. An information session on reverse mortgages with Alan Brewer's face prominently featured on the flyer. They'd be wanting to take that down. Sure enough. Haircuts by Marie Ruiz, Friday mornings from eight to eleven.

"So Marie Ruiz cuts hair here?" I asked, trying to sound nonchalant.

"Yep. She comes in every Friday. The ladies love her. She does a great job, you know?" Arleen said.

"She was here last Friday?" I asked.

Arleen blinked a few times. "As far as I know. I could double-check for you."

"That would be great."

Arleen pulled out a log book and leafed back through it. "Yep. She was here. She cut Olive's hair, did a wash and set for Henrietta, and did a perm for Grace."

Did that truly close her window of opportunity on shooting Alan? Could she have done both? "How long would that have taken her?"

Arleen shrugged. "Three or four hours. Looks like she started a little early that day. Closer to seven thirty. Those perms take time."

Seven thirty. No way could she have shot Alan and been here doing a wash and set by then. Marie was not the culprit. On the other hand, I was going to look awesome for some time to come. I turned just in time to see an older woman march up to the bulletin board, grab down the flyer with Alan's face on it, rip it into four pieces, crumble those up, throw them away, and march off. I'd seen that woman before. I'd seen her when she'd taken a picture of Alan in his casket at his viewing. She'd been dressed up then, but she wasn't now. She had on a pair of loose, flowing pants and a sleeveless top. On her feet, she wore a pair of high-top Chucks with hearts on them.

I might have lost one suspect, but I may have gained another. Whoever it was wasn't crazy about Alan. I froze for a second, unsure of what to do. She walked out of the center, and by the time I rushed out to try to catch her, she was gone. I went back inside and asked Arleen, "Who was that?"

"Tanya Medina," Arleen sighed. "You know, the artist? She keeps ripping those signs down."

"Why?" I asked.

"She lost her house because of one of those reverse mortgages. I don't know the details. I just know that she blamed the bank. Every time they have one of those informational meetings, she pickets outside it."

I pulled the flyer she had ripped up out of the garbage and pieced it back together. The informational meeting was tonight.

I went back outside and called Lola. "Has Tanya Medina ever been in your house?"

There was a pause as she thought. "I think maybe when our house was on the garden tour. It was right after I redid the patio. Yes. Definitely. I remember it now. A bee got tangled up in Tanya's scarf, and I thought her friend Estelle was going to have a heart attack over it."

"Would they have been inside the house?" I asked.

"Yes. Those two came in to get a drink of water and calm down after the bee thing."

My suspect pool was expanding fast. If it got any bigger any faster, I might just drown.

Chapter Twenty

Back home, I skipped upstairs and opened up my laptop. My first search of "Tanya Medina artist Verbena" came up with around five million hits in less than a second. I started clicking. Her Facebook page was set to private. I clicked the button to send her a friend request. It was amazing how many people accepted those automatically. Maybe she would be one of those and I'd have a better sense of who she was and what she was up to. Next up was the website for her art. The first image came up, and I gasped. I knew the view. It was from the ridge where I had hiked with my father so many times. The Mondrian-like patchwork of the farmland stretched away into the distance with the blue sky above it so clear that it might cut. I peered closer. It wasn't huge. Maybe only thirty-six by twenty-four inches. It would fit perfectly in the spot where the girl on the rock had been. The rest of the pieces were gorgeous too, but it was that one that really spoke to me.

Next I clicked on a link to the *Verbena Free Press*.

The Verbena Free Press

WEDNESDAY, OCTOBER 18

Widow Handcuffs Herself to Home

Tanya Medina had to be removed by the police from her home on Tuesday. She had handcuffed herself to the wrought iron railing on the front porch, vowing that she would never leave willingly. The house had gone into fore-closure several months before.

"The bank gave Ms. Medina a full month to satisfy the requirements of the contract," Alan Brewer of the Verbena Union Bank said. "I understand that she's upset, but that doesn't make her above the law."

Ms. Medina claims that the bank gave her late husband, Herman Burdette, a misleading contract and that neither of them fully understood the possible repercussions of signing it. "They're ripping off old people! That's what they're doing!" Ms. Medina said.

Yikes. Chaining yourself to a railing and being forcibly removed by law enforcement was fairly badass. There was something more here, though. There were too many holes in the story. There had to be more to it. Arleen said Tanya picketed all the information meetings on reverse mortgages. Maybe I could find her there and talk to her and find out the rest of the story. Would it be enough to have Tanya do more than spray-paint threats on the bank doors?

I clicked back over to her painting. I really hoped not. That painting was gorgeous.

*   *   *

I pulled up to the Civic Center to attend the information meeting on reverse mortgages that Alan had been meant to give. Four older women sat in camp chairs in the shade holding signs. "Reverse Mortgages Reverse Your Rights." "Know Your Rights. Don't Reverse."

The one that caught my eye read, "Bankers Who Sell Reverses Should Wind Up in Hearses." Beneath the slogan was a photo of Alan Brewer in his casket. It was held by Tanya Medina. I recoiled. The disrespect and the rage it took to make a sign like that shocked me and, frankly, made me a little ill.

As threatening as the sign was, nothing much seemed to be happening. The four women sat calmly in their chairs, signs resting in front of them. One of them was knitting. Then I saw Johanna from the bank pull up. So did my quartet of protestors. They were on their feet in seconds.

Johanna got out of her car, briefcase in hand, and walked toward the Civic Center entrance. The women followed behind her. Tanya yelled, "Stepping into Alan

Brewer's shoes, Johanna? Better watch your step! Karma came for him. It could come for you too!"

Johanna visibly blanched. Her steps faltered, but she swallowed hard, straightened her shoulders, and marched into the Civic Center. The four women went back to their seats and sat down like a Greek chorus awaiting their next cue. I'm no fan of the reverse mortgage. I'd done a story on them back in my reporter days, and they can be terrible for consumers. At the moment, though, they weren't illegal. The bank wasn't doing anything against the law by offering them or even by promoting them. Ethics was another question.

I got out of my car and started up the sidewalk. The quartet of protestors jumped to their feet, then got a good look at me and faltered just like Johanna had, steps slowing to a halting stop. They looked at each other, confused, and then looked back at me.

"Hi," I said. I pointed to the sign with Alan's face on it. "Pretty scary sign."

Tanya looked at me, her eyes narrowed. "You're the Turner girl, aren't you?"

I nodded. "And you're the one who took that photo of Alan when he was at my family's funeral home."

"It's not illegal," she said, a smirk on her face. "I looked it up."

It wasn't. There were times when people took photos of the deceased in caskets. Usually, it was to send to relatives who couldn't attend the funeral. It still gave me a bit of the heebie-jeebies. It reminded me too much of those creepy Victorian photos with parents propping up their dead children. "Neither are reverse mortgages," I said with a matching smirk.

She looked up at me, one eye squinted shut. "You're a bit of a smartass, aren't you?"

I shrugged. "Better than being a dumbass."

She cackled and pulled out her phone. "I'm accepting your friend request."

"Gosh, thanks." I pointed to her sign again. "You took that photo just to make a sign to scare other bankers?"

"I took it for myself so I could always see that he was dead, that at least I'd have the satisfaction of outliving him." She smiled. "The sign was a bonus."

I shook my head. "That's a lot of hate you're holding onto."

She laughed. "I'm not holding onto it, honey. I'm sending it out into the universe. As far as I'm concerned, I'd be fine if that hate helped bring him down."

One of her friends touched her leg. "Tanya, enough. You're going too far. Again."

"He lost me my house!" she shouted back at her friend. "Did he go too far?"

Her friend pressed her lips together. "You know he did. That's why we're all here. So that what happened to you doesn't happen to anyone else."

Now things were getting interesting. "What happened?"

The story was long and a little convoluted. Tanya had met Herman Burdette when he hired her to paint a portrait of his beagle. Along with casket photography, pet portraiture was one of Tanya's specialties. In the process of working on the painting, they got to know each other and fell in love. As one does. Nothing like pet portraiture to get the juices flowing, I guess.

"How does that relate to reverse mortgages?" I asked.

"Herman took out a reverse mortgage on the house. You know, so we'd have a little extra cash to travel and things like that." Tanya put her hand on her heart. "Such a dear man. We had such wonderful special times. Take a look at my Facebook page. You'll see the photos of all the adventures we went on."

"Okay," I said, hoping we were getting somewhere.

"Tanya's name couldn't be on the mortgage because she was under sixty-five," her friend explained.

I knew enough about reverse mortgages to suspect where this was heading and got a bad feeling in my stomach.

"Herman died. Quite unexpectedly. He'd been a really healthy, vigorous man in his late sixties, but when he was out weeding the garden, he dropped dead. Poof." Tanya made a bursting motion with her hands. "Just like that."

"I'm so sorry," I said.

"My name wasn't on the deed to the house, but I was Herman's heir. The bank gave me thirty days to pay off the balance of the loan. When I couldn't pay it off, they foreclosed on me." Tears welled up in her eyes.

I didn't blame her. I'd heard stories like this one, but it still seemed draconian to kick a woman out of her house a month after her husband died because of a technicality on the paperwork. "It was Alan who made that decision? The one to foreclose?"

Tanya nodded.

"That had to be some pretty bad publicity for the bank." The article I'd read hadn't been too bad, but kicking widows out of their homes wasn't really what good neighborhood banks did.

"Have you heard of banks getting good publicity?" Tanya asked. "They don't care anymore. Saying a bank did something wrong is a little like saying that Satan sinned. It's not news."

"Tanya will be okay," her friend said, putting a hand on Tanya's arm. "She's got us. She's got enough money to live on, but what about other people? We wanted to put a little fear into the hearts of people like Alan Brewer."

I pointed at the sign. "That's more than a little fear."

Tanya waved it away. "It's just a sign. Besides, what could an old lady do?"

"An old lady can shoot a gun," I said. Tanya was a straight shooter in conversation. Was she one in real life too? Whoever hit Alan with that bullet either had great luck or great aim.

Tanya reared back. "You think I shot Alan over my eviction? That's ridiculous. Besides, they've arrested the man who did it."

"*Allegedly* did it," I corrected. Why didn't people get that distinction? "I don't think he did, though."

She thought for a moment. "It is hard to believe someone with that touch with roses would kill someone. Who do you think did it?" she asked.

I ignored her question. "Did you? You've been to Kyle and Lola's house when it was on the garden tour. You could know where they kept their gun." Might as well get straight to the point. I turned to her friends. "Or did one of you do it?"

They all laughed as if I'd told a really good joke.

"What?" I asked, feeling foolish and not entirely sure why.

She gestured to me. "Go check my Facebook page. You'll see."

I took a step back and pulled out my phone, pulling up Facebook. Sure enough, Tanya Medina had accepted my friend request. I went to her page.

"Go to the photos albums. Look at the one called 'Cruise,'" Tanya directed me.

I did. The cover photo showed three women standing under a banner that read, "Welcome to Ensenada—July 12."

"We were on a three-day cruise to Ensenada. Fabulous food. You ought to go," Tanya said.

"Anybody can fake a date on a photo," I said. "That's not enough."

She waved a hand at me. "Call the cruise line and ask around. People tend to notice us."

So another suspect cleared. I was clearing everybody but Kyle. I looked at my phone again. Next to the album for the cruise was one called "Paintings." I clicked that open and found the one that had taken my breath away. I turned the phone toward Tanya. "Tell me about this."

She squinted at my phone. "Oh, it's part of my local landscape series."

"You have more than one of them?" I asked.

Her friend cackled. "More like fifteen of them. And counting."

"Do you sell them?" I asked.

*   *   *

After making a handshake deal on Tanya's painting of the view from Cold Clutch Canyon, I went inside to talk to Johanna. She jumped a little as I walked in. She looked rattled. It couldn't have been easy to walk past those signs, and apparently it was taking a toll on her.

"They're gone. It's probably safe to come out. I don't think anyone else is showing up, though. They're a pretty intense deterring force," I said, looking at her tabletop display of brochures on reverse mortgages.

"That sign with the picture of Alan." She shuddered. "Terrifying."

"They're pretty angry," I said. I didn't fully blame them. "Did the bank really kick Tanya out of her house a month after her husband died?"

Johanna sighed. "I wasn't in on those decisions. The reverse mortgage program was really Alan's thing. He promoted it, managed it, and made all those choices. It does seem . . . harsh."

"Decisions plural?" I asked. Had Alan foreclosed on more than one widow? That wasn't exactly a way to make friends.

"I can't really discuss that." She started packing up her display.

Couldn't or wouldn't? I wondered. "Are you going to continue the program?"

She shook her head. "Alan had this session already scheduled, so I filled in, but I'm not going to set up any more." She gestured around to the empty room. "There's not much point, is there?"

There might not have been a point to the promotional meeting, but there definitely was a point for me to look into. How many people had lost their houses because of decisions Alan had made about reverse mortgages?

I said good-bye and went outside. I pulled out my cell and called Jasmine. "What are you doing?"

"What am I always doing?" she countered.

I thought for a second. "Listening to other people's problems, usually. You generally don't answer your phone when you're doing that, though."

"True. I'm finished listening to people's problems, and now I'm writing case files about listening to people's problems."

"Great. I'll be right over." I strolled past Tappiano's and the Clean Green Car Wash, where a group of guys in matching polo shirts sat in the shade not washing cars. Where did they get the moldy money they were depositing at the bank? No one ever seemed to be there getting their car washed except Professor Moonbeam, and they weren't exactly doing a bang-up job on his truck. Oh, wait. There was one person. Rosemarie came out as they pulled her Mercedes out front. She took the key from one of the men, got in, and drove away. I waved to her, but apparently she didn't see me.

A small group of people were leaving the building that housed Jasmine's office. Mostly men. I only recognized one. Professor Moonbeam in his kurta getting into his dirty truck and driving away. Another one looked familiar too. I couldn't quite place where I'd seen him or why he seemed familiar, though. Something about his walk. I waited for the group to disperse, then I walked in and plopped down in the comfy chair across from Jasmine.

"Do we know anybody who went into real estate?" I asked.

"Are you kidding me?" she asked.

"No."

"Have you not looked at the little divider things at Al's Fine Foods? Or the cup sleeves over at Cup o' Joe's? Or the bus stop at Sparrow and Goldfinch?"

I was usually pretty observant. None of those things had tripped any of my triggers, though. "Why?"

"Michelle Swanson's face is on every single one of those things. Everywhere. Ready to help if you're interested in buying or selling a home," Jasmine said in a mock singsong voice.

Michelle Swanson had been a cheerleader at Verbena High, but not a particularly obnoxious one. Actually, contrary to every teen movie ever made, the cheerleaders from our year were never obnoxious or cliquey. A little bubblier than I generally could stand, but whose fault was that? "So I bet her phone number and e-mail address are on all those things too."

"They wouldn't exactly be a good marketing tool otherwise."

"Excellent."

"Why do you need to talk to someone in real estate? You looking to buy?" She snorted at the thought.

"No. Just trying to find some information on people who've lost their houses recently."

"Why?"

"Because people like that might have a grudge against a banker," I said.

Jasmine paused. "Could be."

Chapter Twenty-One

The Verbena Free Press

SUNDAY, JULY 21

Annual Fire Festival Scheduled for July 26

The Verbena Fire Festival and Street Fair will take place on Friday, July 26, between Oriole and Robin Streets from 4 PM to 10 PM. The fair will feature performances by the Verbena Ballet School and the Verbena High Marching Band. Cold Clutch Canyon Café's food truck will be serving steak Diane and bananas Foster, and Tappiano's has developed special fiery sangrias for the occasion. Many area businesses will have booths with games and information. Fireworks start at 9:30 PM by the gazebo.

The Fire Festival celebrates the fire of 1913 that nearly demolished the town of Verbena. Instead of walking away, the citizens of Verbena came together to rebuild their beloved town. The Fire Festival celebrates that spirit.

* * *

Michelle was easy to reach and easy to schedule an appointment with. She answered on the second ring. She at least pretended to remember who I was and pretended to be enthusiastic about seeing me. "Come by the house on Monday," she said. "We can catch up."

I contained the sigh that rose up in me like a reflex to that phrase. "Great," I said instead.

She gave me the address, and the next morning, I drove over there. It was in a new area of Verbena. Another change since I'd left. There hadn't been houses like these when I'd lived here: two-story stucco minimansions with faux Palladian windows and lawns the size of postage stamps. I glanced up and down the street. There were three models and about four colors. They were mixed enough that it didn't quite look like ticky-tacky houses from the old folk song, but the underlying sentiment sure was there. The sidewalk sparkled in the sunlight. I rang the bell. Tasteful chimes ensued, then the door flew open.

"If it isn't the flavor of the week!" Michelle said, taking a moment to look me up and down. She gave me a quick hug and an air kiss and said, "Your hair looks great. Come on in out of that heat, Desiree."

I stepped into the cool air-conditioned tile foyer, wondering when Michelle had become a southerner and what the flavor-of-the-week comment meant. It took my eyes a few seconds to adjust from the glaring sunlight outside. The ceiling soared above me, a chandelier floating from it. Stairs wound up to the second floor. The walls were dark sage green and the ceiling sparkling white. There wasn't a cobweb in sight. "Your home is beautiful."

She gave a coy little smile. "In this case, the cobbler's children have nice shoes. It's a marketing tool all on its own." She motioned for me to follow her. "Let's go settle in the family room. We'll be comfy in there."

I love the Turner Family Funeral Home, but it's old. It's another building that went up right after the fire of 1913, and it has Frank Lloyd Wright's influence written all over it. It had style, but that style was dated, and the upstairs in particular could use a fresh coat of paint and a serious update of the kitchen. This house screamed the kind of California you see on television. High ceilings. Big windows. Tile floors. All of it cool and clean. We stepped down into the big family room/kitchen. We did the usual catch-up dance. Michelle had a little boy who looked so much like his father that I wasn't sure Michelle had passed on any genetic material whatsoever. He was at a playdate at the moment, so she had just thirty minutes to explain whatever it was I wanted her to explain to me.

"Would you be able to tell if someone had lost their home because of a reverse mortgage?" I asked.

"You mean like would there be some sort of sign on them? Like a scarlet *M*?" She tucked her feet up underneath her on the big leather couch.

I laughed. "No. I mean, would there be something in some kind of database that might clue you in?"

She tapped her forefinger against her lower lip as she thought. "Probably nothing that specific. I could definitely find out if a house had gone into foreclosure. Then you could probably backtrack from there, but it would have to be on a case-by-case basis."

That could be time consuming. "How many foreclosures would you say there are around Verbena?"

She smoothed back her already smooth blonde hair. "It happens. It's not like it was ten years ago when the bottom dropped out of the real estate market and half the state was underwater on their mortgages. Things have bounced back since then. Still, people fall on hard times. Lose a job. Get sick. Get divorced. Suddenly, they can't pay their mortgage and poof! There goes their house."

"Poof? That sounds a little harsh." It wasn't a magic trick. It was most people's life savings. Then I remembered Tanya Medina's "poof!" about her husband.

"It depends on the lender. Some of them are a little more hardcore than others. There are quite a few who will work with people to keep them in their home. They don't really want the hassle of putting a house into foreclosure and then selling it." She inspected her French manicure.

I tucked my hands under my thighs to hide my nails. "What about the Verbena Union Bank? Are they hardcore?"

Her lips pressed together into a hard, straight line, and she didn't say anything.

"That bad?" I asked.

"I didn't say anything." She pointed out.

Once again, what people didn't say was even more important than what they did say. "But don't they have the reputation of being a friendly hometown bank?"

"They have commercials saying they're a friendly hometown bank. You can say lots of things in commercials." She shrugged. "They actually used to be pretty nice to deal with. Starting a year or so ago, they've gotten a lot more hard line."

This was interesting. Everything seemed to have changed about a year ago. What was the catalyst, though? "Have any of your clients had trouble with them?"

Michelle shook her head. "No. I've steered them elsewhere for their mortgages. Plus I really try not to push people to buy above their means. It doesn't feel right. I like to sleep at night."

A realtor with a conscience. That was nice. "So how would I start getting a list of properties that have been foreclosed on in the last year or so?"

Her eyes narrowed. "Why do you want to know?"

I considered my options. I could lie, but I'm not the best at doing that. I could pretend I was working on a story about reverse mortgages and foreclosures, but who would I say I was writing for? I decided to go with a radical option and tell the truth. "I don't think Kyle Hansen killed Alan Brewer. I'm looking for other people who might have wanted Alan dead. Someone he foreclosed on might be just the ticket."

She sat very still for a second. "Have you talked to Tanya Medina?"

I nodded. "She was on a cruise when it happened."

Michelle made a face. "Too bad. She really had it in for Alan."

"I thought that maybe someone else might also have it in for him and not have been quite so public about it. So what do you say? Will you help me find a list of properties that have been foreclosed on?" I asked. "Please?"

She didn't answer right away.

"Pretty please with a cherry on top?" I said.

"No cherries. I wouldn't mind some wine, though. Tappiano's got this killer rosé, but it's hard to get. They didn't make much. Score me a bottle of that and I'll get you your list. You're still tight with Jasmine, right? I've heard she has a stash." She arched her brows.

"Let me check." I texted Jasmine: "Need a bottle of Tappiano rosé. Can I get?"

She texted back: "Why?"

Me: "Getting Michelle to access database."

Jasmine: "It will cost you."

I turned back to Michelle. "You got it." I'd figure out what I'd owe Jasmine later.

She walked over to the desk in the corner of the room and opened her laptop. "Okay, then. Let's get started. You want the foreclosures in Verbena in the past year, right?"

"For a start." I followed to look over her shoulder, because that always helps people work more efficiently.

She tapped on her computer keyboard and then said, "Here you go. That's what's in foreclosure or in danger of being foreclosed on right now." She turned the monitor to face me. There were ten listings.

No names or addresses jumped out at me. "What about ones that have already been purchased by someone else?"

"Once the property has changed hands, the notice of default would be gone," she said.

I leaned against the desk. "Is there any way to go backward and find that information?"

"Not on the computer, but I keep some hard copies of listings." She turned away from the laptop.

I sat back upright. "You do?"

"Yeah. I like to know who my competition is. I'll go back to check occasionally if someone bought a property I'm interested in. Sometimes you can see patterns in things when they're printed out more easily than on the screen." She tapped the computer.

"Can I see some of those listings?" I asked.

She hauled a three-ring binder off the bookshelf to her right and plopped it down in front of me. I leafed through it, not entirely sure what I was looking for. *Patterns*, Michelle had said. She looked for patterns. I tried squinting my eyes to see if something would jump out at me like one of those Magic Eye posters. Shockingly, something did. Several of the properties in danger of foreclosure listed in one of the months weren't in town. They were out on the county roads.

"How come so many properties out in the country were suddenly listed?" I asked.

"King Snake Fire," she said.

I looked again at the date. "Oh, yeah." It had been about that time. My dad had still been alive. I'd still had a job in the career of my choice. The hills I'd loved hadn't burned to a cinder because of some teenager with illegal fireworks. Good times. "But why would that have put places into foreclosure? Wouldn't they have been insured?"

"Sometimes insurance doesn't cover everything or is slow to get people a check. Or maybe the people don't have the heart to rebuild and decide it's easier to let it go." She looked a little sad. I was starting to think Michelle actually cared about people being in homes they liked.

I pointed to the row of them in the listing. "Were any of these purchased?"

"I can check." She opened the laptop and tapped at her keyboard again, then plunked her finger on the first one. "This one didn't sell. The owners must have gotten caught up on their payments. This one sold, though, and for cheap." She touched the next one.

"Who's the new owner?"

She tapped some more and then made a face. "Monique Woodall."

"Monique, the waitress from the café?" That made no sense.

Michelle shrugged. "Unless there's another Monique Woodall in town, it's her. Smart girl. I can see her investing in real estate."

"How on earth could a waitress afford to buy a property like that? Or should I be asking how good the tips at the café are?" Maybe I should see if I could pick up a couple of shifts.

Michelle shook her head. "She might not have needed that much. It's a pretty hefty loan. She financed ninety percent of the purchase price."

"What would she be doing with a piece of property like that?" This still wasn't connecting up for me.

Michelle shrugged. "An investment maybe? Rental property? If so, she's shrewder than she looks."

"Do people rent out rural properties like that?" I asked. I'd always thought of those places as family farms.

"Sure."

"What about some of these other properties?"

Ten minutes later, Michelle said, "Monique bought four of these properties."

"Flabbergasted" is the best description I can come up with for how I was feeling. Gobsmacked, perhaps, too. "Four? How could she possibly afford that?" Even with financing, the down payments would be substantial.

Michelle peered into the screen. "I don't think she did it alone."

"Who helped? Her parents?" I didn't think they had anywhere near that amount of money either.

Michelle sat back in her chair. "Alan Brewer cosigned on all four loans."

Alan and Monique? My mind began to race. Monique had that same honey-blonde hair as Christine, Marie, Trixie Warner, Ella Keller, and Mandy Smith. The color that Rosemarie had dyed hers to be. Could Monique be in line to be the next entrepreneur that Alan was helping finance her dreams? Or maybe she was in line to be the next Mrs. Brewer? Easy terms on a loan were one thing. Huge chunks of cash invested in property were another. What had I heard Christine saying at the funeral? That she always thought there was more money hidden somewhere? Was Alan buying things in Monique's name to hide assets from Rosemarie? Had he done the same thing to Christine?

We are all creatures of habit. It's the way most of us are hardwired. We like the rhythm and order of routine. Maybe Alan's routine was to trade in one wife for another every few years and to take as much of his money with him as he could. Had it led to his death?

"Thanks, Michelle." I closed up the binders. "This has been very helpful."

"No problem at all." She grabbed her purse and walked to the door with me.

"So what was that flavor-of-the-week crack about?" I asked.

"Seriously?" She laughed.

"Yeah, seriously."

"Well, let's see. Nate Johar is moping around like someone kicked his dog. You're on the front page of the *Free Press* every other day. Luke Butler chases you to Tappiano's every chance he gets. That all pretty much started when you came back to town."

I blushed. I hadn't thought of any of it like that. Flavor of the week, huh?

Chapter Twenty-Two

I took the addresses of the four properties and went look-ing to see what Monique had purchased. It was a gor-geous day for a drive. The sky soared above me, blue and blank. The hills in the distance looked golden and soft, dot-ted with clumps of green live oak. I knew up close they'd be sunstruck brown grass, but it didn't stop me from admiring the beautiful golden shades against the blue sky. The map program on my phone told me to turn off the highway onto a county road. I followed it for about a mile, then the road took a hard left. I stayed with it. After a series of three more zigs and at least one zag, I turned into a driveway and then stopped. A substantial gate rose in front of me.

I got out and tugged on the gate. It wasn't budging. Then I noticed the rather substantial lock it had to go with its height and breadth.

Lots of people out here fenced their properties. But six-foot-high fences? Not so much. With fences come gates, but *locked* gates? Also not so typical. Kyle and Lola were much more the norm with their lack of locks. I peered through the bars but couldn't see much. Someone had planted oleanders along the fence line. Oleanders grow like weeds in Northern California. They need next to no water and make great privacy breaks. Plus they have pretty flowers. Poisonous as hell, but as long as you're not in the habit of munching on your landscaping, it doesn't matter too much. It's why you see them on so many highway medians and along so many properties. At any rate, these oleanders were doing just fine, with glossy green leaves and sprays of delicate pink flowers. They were pretty much all I could see. What I could see didn't look so great. In fact, it looked an awful lot like the areas around my favorite hike that were coming back from the fire. Black scorched soil with a few shoots of green coming through. So Michelle was right. This property was one that had been burned in the King Snake Fire and then sold rather than rebuilt. But what the heck was Monique doing with it? She certainly wasn't living on it, and if anyone else was, they hadn't gotten around to landscaping anything but the fence line.

I got in my car and drove to the second property on my list. Another fence. Another gate. Another lock. More oleanders. On the third address, though, I got a better look at what was inside. The oleanders planted along the edge of the property hadn't been doing quite as well as they had at the others. I could only see the corner of the structure at the top of the driveway, but it was enough to figure out what it was: a greenhouse.

I walked back to the Element, kicking at the gravel of the driveway, and opened the door. Before I could get in, a dirt-spattered pickup truck pulled into the drive next to me. I hesitated, torn between getting more information and possibly getting into a confrontation. The man who jumped out of the truck didn't seem very threatening. Something about the pajamas and that whole slightly-hunched-shoulder thing made me think I could take him if push came to shove. "Can I help you?" Professor Moonbeam asked.

I smiled. "No, I was just curious. Something about big fences and gates makes me want to know what's on the other side."

He smiled back. "A questioning mind. I understand. Want to see inside?"

I hesitated again. Was it a ploy? Was he going to hit me on the head with a shovel once we were out of sight? I decided I'd make sure not to walk in front of him and said, "Sure."

He unlocked the gate and slid it open, then motioned for me to follow him. The smell hit me pretty much about ten yards in. There's a reason they call it skunkweed.

"Wow," I said.

"Oh," he said. "You mean the smell. Yeah. You get used to it after a while. I barely smell it anymore."

"You're around it that much?" I asked.

"Pretty much every day, all day." He stuck out his hand. "Kevin Moonbeam, by the way."

"Desiree Turner," I said back, shaking his hand.

"I know. From the funeral home. The prodigal who has returned." He turned and kept walking up the drive. "I read about you from time to time in the newspaper."

Well, that was embarrassing. If I'd had any illusions that everyone wasn't talking about me, they were gone now. We were only about ten steps closer to the greenhouse when a man emerged from behind it with a rifle slung casually over his forearm. "Whoa, whoa, whoa!" I said, backing up.

Moonbeam held up his hands. "It's okay, David. I invited her in."

David didn't say anything. He looked from Moonbeam to me and back again. "You sure?"

"Completely."

David went back where he came from, and I relaxed my sphincters. "Kind of heavy artillery for a greenhouse, don't you think?" Something bothered me, though. I could have sworn I'd seen David before. Of course, at first, he was nothing but the big gun he'd handled so casually. I'd seen almost nothing else. Once Moonbeam calmed the situation, though? Then I was sure I'd seen him before. I just wasn't sure where.

He held his hands out to the sides. "I'm afraid it's a necessary evil of the moment. We're getting near harvest, and poachers are a problem." He motioned to some trees to the side of the driveway. "Let's get out of the heat."

I followed him to the shade. "Why the marijuana business?"

Professor Moonbeam ran his hand over his face. "My mother died."

I pulled up short. "I'm so sorry."

He held up his hand. "It was years ago. Long before I left the university. Cancer."

I stood still and waited. There was more to the story. Sometimes you had to wait for people to be ready to tell you.

"She spent her last weeks either in terrible pain or so drugged that she didn't know where she was or who any of us were. She was a wonderful woman. Smart. Creative. Funny. It still hurts me to think of how much pain she was in. It hurts me even more to know that it wasn't necessary." There was a sadness in his face that was truly heartbreaking.

"What could they have done?" I asked.

"Marijuana can provide an amazing amount of pain relief without the side effects of opiates." He took a deep breath. "I can only imagine what my mother's last days would have been like if she'd had access to that kind of palliative care. I want to be sure that no one else has to go through what she went through."

I nodded. "So you decided to start developing medical marijuana?"

"Exactly. I started doing research on specific strains and began to develop my own. It's an amazing plant." He gestured for me to follow him to the greenhouse and opened the door and peeked in. It was thick with beautiful, lush, green plants, but the smell had me taking steps back.

"You didn't feel you could stay at the university and do this work?" I asked.

He shook his head. "Too many rules. Too many regulations. The constant scrambling for grant money, for position, for power."

"Lots of money involved in the cannabis trade," I observed. "It didn't have anything to do with that?"

He shrugged. "Sure. I like my creature comforts as much as the next guy. It's not the only goal I have for my work, though."

I looked around at the greenhouse and irrigation system. "It couldn't have been cheap to get started, though, right? That must have taken some money upfront."

"Luckily, there are people who understand that this is just the beginning for the cannabis industry and are willing to invest in one man's dream." He smiled.

"Isn't the money stuff pretty complicated still?" I asked.

"Very." He gestured around the property. "This here? This is all legal in the state of California and in Pluma

Vista County. It's not legal on the federal level, though. I think the feds will eventually catch up to the rest of the country. Your grandchildren will hear stories about the legalization of marijuana and think about it the same way you probably think about prohibition."

"How do you get around that now, though?" I asked.

His smiled faded a bit. "That's an area I'd rather not discuss too much. Let's just say that there are ways around things."

"Not even a hint?" I pressed.

"No, young lady. Not even a hint." His face became more serious. "Now, if you don't mind, I need to get to work."

"Sure. Thanks for the tour." I headed back to the gate, got back into the Element, and drove away.

I called Jasmine on my way home. "You are not going to believe this."

"I am a therapist," she said. "You would not believe eighty percent of what I know about this town. What's more, you wouldn't want to believe it. People are crazy, and that's a professional opinion."

"It keeps you in business," I pointed out.

"True. Now what is it I'm not going to believe?"

I explained what I'd found out at Michelle's and what I'd found at the different properties. "It explains Monique's shoes," I said.

"Her shoes?"

"Yeah. At the memorial service, I thought she was wearing Louboutins, but then I decided she couldn't be. How could she afford that? Now I know."

"That doesn't make sense either," Jasmine said. "If she has enough money for Louboutins, why is she still pulling double shifts at Cold Clutch Canyon Café and Tappiano's?"

I didn't have an answer to those questions. "I don't know, but I'm going to find out."

"How? When?"

I glanced at the dashboard clock. "I'm not sure and tomorrow. I've got Jamal Pitt's service in about an hour."

"You sure you want to do that?" she asked.

"I'm not sure I've got a lot of choice. Donna's still on bed rest, and you know how awful Uncle Joey can be at a service." He had a tendency to cry.

She hesitated. "One more thing . . ."

"What?" I asked.

"Be careful around Moonbeam, okay?"

Then it hit me. I'd seen him coming out of her office on a Saturday. He was part of her anger management group. It hardly seemed possible. "Moonbeam? He's a creampuff. He's all about relieving people's pain and doing good in the world. I'm way more worried about his friend with the rifle." I shuddered a bit thinking of how casually David carried that rifle.

"Just remember that appearances can be deceiving."

Chapter Twenty-Three

The Verbena Free Press

MONDAY, JULY 22

Firework Safety Reminder

Detective Luke Butler of the Verbena Police Department
wants to remind citizens that while there will be fireworks
at the Fire Festival, it is still illegal for private citizens to
light fireworks themselves.

"No one wants a repeat of the King Snake Fire of 2015,"
he said. "Leave the fireworks to the professionals."

So Monique owned the land that Professor Moonbeam
was farming marijuana on. Alan Brewer had cosigned
on the loans and was a banker who might well know
some ways around the regulations that made money such
an issue for entrepreneurs like Moonbeam. It was quite
the cozy arrangement. Cozy arrangements can go terribly

wrong sometimes, though. You had money and drugs and sex all rolled up together. I took my laptop into the kitchen and settled down at the table with some cookies I found in the cupboard. First, I went into the program that let me monitor the motion-sensitive security camera I'd installed on our back porch, the back porch where someone had left that yarn and the charm for Donna. Sure enough, there was Uncle Joey coming in from bowling at about eleven. And a squirrel that I could swear was mocking me an hour after that. That was it.

Next, I typed "marijuana and banking" into the search engine. I was blasted with pages and pages of information. I narrowed it by adding California into the search. There were still reams of information. It took a few hours to sort through, but it eventually boiled down to this: there was no good way for marijuana growers and dispensary owners to bank their money. Banks were federally insured, and marijuana was still illegal under federal law. Banks couldn't knowingly open an account for someone who was getting that money through illegal means.

People resorted to all kinds of different measures to get around it all. One person who was interviewed said he'd actually buried his money around his property in different places and had kept a map of all the spots so he wouldn't lose any of it. "I felt like a pirate with a treasure map," he'd said. Money that had been buried would smell funny, wouldn't it? Damp gets into a lot of places even when you think you've sealed it up tight. Just ask any coffin maker. Rosemarie had given me a pile of moldy cash that Alan had stashed in his own personal safe. Could he have been skimming some of the profits from the marijuana business? That could have soured the relationship between him and Moonbeam.

There was a lot of money to be made in marijuana these days. Other people found ways to launder the money, and a few simply carried around sacks full of cash.

Then I did a little research on Professor Moonbeam. The name change made it a little tricky, but only a little. Professor Moonbeam was originally Professor Grady Hammon. Four years ago, he had taken a hoe to the windshield of his department head's Prius after a dispute over greenhouse space with another faculty member. That had earned him probation. Two years later, he had used a soil cultivator to break into another lab when he thought they'd taken supplies he'd ordered for his own lab. A pattern was emerging: Someone who solved his problems with violence. Someone who was growing marijuana on land owned by Alan Brewer. He smashed up a car over greenhouse space. What might he have done if he thought someone was stealing money from him? What had Luke said about the marijuana business? Someone was going to get shot? Well, someone definitely had been shot. Was it because of his involvement in the marijuana business?

I picked up the phone and called Lola. "Hey, about that garden tour thing you mentioned . . . you said all kinds of gardeners were on it, right? Not just rose growers?" Marijuana was a plant. Somebody interested in plants might well go on a garden tour.

"Right," she said.

"Do you remember Professor Moonbeam being on it?" I asked.

She laughed. "It's hard to forget Professor Moonbeam. He sent me a poem about the rose arbor about a week later. So sweet."

Yeah. Sweet. "Do you see him around your area much?" The greenhouses weren't far from Lola and Kyle's place, but they weren't exactly right next door.

"Not me. Let me check with Kyle." I heard her call the question to Kyle, and then he got on the phone.

"I've seen him out in the morning sometimes. He does this thing where he clasps his hands behind his back and sort of bends forward as he walks. Always looks like he's walking into a stiff headwind."

So he'd been to Lola and Kyle's house. He might know Kyle's walking habits. I thanked Kyle and we hung up.

Donna came into the kitchen, yarn and crochet hook clutched to her chest. "What are you working on?"

"I'm solving Alan Brewer's murder." I smiled up at her. It was good to see her up and moving around a bit. She'd stopped moping too. "It's all tied up with Monique Woodall and marijuana."

"Monique is growing marijuana?" Donna asked.

"Not exactly. She owns the property that someone else is growing the marijuana on and has some kind of business interest in it. I've been trying to get to the bottom of it to clear Kyle."

Donna shook her head like there was something in her ear. "What does Alan Brewer have to do with any of it? Did this entire town go to hell in a handbasket in the few short days I was on bed rest?"

"Close to it. I'm pretty sure Alan had everything to do with it. He cosigned the loans for Monique. Moonbeam said something about forward-thinking investors giving him the seed money to get started, as it were. I think it's possible that Alan was footing the bills for a lot of the start-up expenses. Plus, right now, the most difficult part of the whole business is the money thing. No one can put the money into a bank account because marijuana is still illegal on a federal level. Who better to figure out ways around that than a banker? Especially a banker like Alan, who was always looking for an angle." Someone who would exploit old people to make a buck wouldn't think twice about getting into the marijuana business.

Donna tapped her finger against her lips. "So what would he have to do with the money to make it so it could go into the bank?"

"Launder it, I suppose." That was the step I hadn't quite figured out yet. It was complicated.

"How do you do that?" she asked.

"I don't know the fine points of it, but you have to find a way to make it look like the money is coming from a respectable source. Some kind of place that does a lot of cash business." At least those were the basics of it.

"What around here is like that? There've been a bunch of new businesses opening up in the past year or so." Donna picked up her crochet hook. At least she'd slowed down on the baby-blanket production since the doctor had given the okay for her to make videos and programs and do some of the bookkeeping tasks that I sucked at.

The Dollar General, the In-n-Out, the flower shop, the gym, and the bookkeeper were all new. None of them seemed likely to generate enough cash business to work. Suddenly, I sat up straight. "The car wash!"

Donna looked confused for a moment. "The Clean Green Car Wash?"

"Yeah! No one would think twice if a car wash had a lot of cash business. And there's hardly ever anybody there." Hadn't I seen Professor Moonbeam going in and out of there regularly, and yet his truck was always crusted with dirt? Maybe he wasn't there for a car wash at all. Maybe he was dropping off money to be laundered rather than dropping off his truck to be washed.

"Don't you think that's a little on the nose? Cash laundering in a car wash?" Donna laughed.

"Sometimes the obvious answer is the right one. Do you know who owns it?" I asked.

Her brow furrowed. "No. I figured it was a chain. How would you find out?"

"Easy peasy. It's public information." I brought up the website for the California secretary of state. I tapped in a few search criteria, and in about five seconds, we had our answer. "Well, butter my butt and call me a biscuit."

"Who? Who owns it?" She poked at me with her foot.

I turned the laptop so she could see. Monique Wood-all owned the Clean Green Car Wash.

She gasped. "That makes perfect sense."

"It sure does. Monique would have to own it to make it all work and to keep the money hidden from Rosemarie and to keep Alan's lily-white hands out of it." The whole scheme was becoming clear in my mind. Alan wanted to leave Rosemarie, but he didn't want to split things down the middle with her. So instead he found sneaky ways to put the money from his new business venture with Moonbeam in Monique's name. What I didn't know was how much Monique knew about it.

What had the teller at the bank said about the musty-smelling money that Rosemarie had found in her safe? The money she thought Alan had left to pay for something in an emergency? He'd said that it smelled like the money from the employees at the car wash. I tapped another search into the computer. If Moonbeam and Alan were using the car wash to launder the marijuana money, that would explain that mildew smell of their money too. Maybe Moonbeam buried it for a while until he could start moving it through the laundering system.

I brought up the website for the car wash. Its cover photo was of the building with a lot of the employees in their matching polo shirts in front. Well, I finally knew where I'd seen David before. He was smack-dab in the middle of the group shot.

"So who else knows about Alan's involvement?" Donna asked.

I thought about it. "No one except Moonbeam. And Monique."

"And you. Who knows that Monique was sleeping with Alan?" Donna asked.

"No one except Monique and Alan."

"And you," she added.

"Yeah, well, but I figured it out after the fact."

Donna stared at me. "Moonbeam has probably figured out that part too by now, right?"

"I'm not sure." I rubbed at my chin. "I think I need to ask some questions and find out."

*   *   *

I didn't know where Monique lived. I didn't know where she hung out. I didn't know what she did for entertainment, but I knew exactly where she'd be on any given weekday morning: waiting tables at the Cold Clutch Canyon Café. I had a sudden hankering for steel-cut oatmeal.

The Cold Clutch has been around since forever, and it's been a pretty decent diner for most of that time. It's open only for breakfast and lunch, no dinner. Grilled cheese, burgers, Monte Cristo sandwiches, Cobb salads, milk shakes. All solid. All dependable.

Then Dolores and Alfonso Molina moved to town. They bought the café from Freddie Koontz, who was ready to retire, and then they promptly closed the place for renovations. You would have thought they'd closed access to oxygen by the way people reacted. Then word started getting around. They'd hired some fancy cabinetmaker from the Bay Area to do the carpentry work. They'd bought all their appliances through Wolf and Sub-Zero. They were going to make the place into one of those fancy-ass restaurants where you paid twenty-eight dollars for one mushroom stuffed with crab on a little puddle of sauce.

There was a little confusion when they reopened. Things didn't seem all that different. The booths were all in the same place, but the cracked vinyl had been replaced. The pies still were displayed in a glass case, but it appeared to be refrigerated. Even the menu was the same, but different. There were still grilled cheese, burgers, milk shakes, and Monte Cristo sandwiches. The difference came in how they were prepared. Everything was now locally sourced, organic, and fresh. Nothing from cans. Nothing from the freezer. Everything was delicious. I wasn't sure what they did to the oatmeal, but it was amazing. Creamy and rich and sweet.

I went in and asked for a booth, which would put me in Monique's section. She came over with a menu and a coffeepot.

"Yes, please," I said, turning over my cup. "Did your shoes recover from Alan's funeral?"

"What?" She stopped pouring.

"I noticed you'd gotten mud on them. People don't realize how soft the ground can be at a cemetery. It's always better to wear flats." I shrugged. "Or wedge heels. Wedges work great. Stilettos? Not so much. Anyway, I hope you were able to clean them. I'd hate to see such an expensive pair of shoes ruined."

"How do you know they were expensive?" Her eyes narrowed as she looked at me.

"I saw the red soles, Monique. If you don't want people to know you're rocking Louboutins, don't flash those soles around. I'm probably not the only one who recognizes that kind of thing around here." Living in Los Angeles had made me more style conscious than most of the people around Verbena were, but fashionistas existed everywhere.

She turned nearly as red as the sole of her shoes had been. "What do you want?"

"Steel-cut oatmeal and to know what your relationship with Alan Brewer was." I shut the menu and handed it to her.

"I served Alan lunch three times a week." She finished pouring my coffee and made a note in her pad. "Brown sugar and bananas or berries with raw sugar on your oatmeal?"

"Brown sugar and bananas . . . and really? That's it? Lunch three times a week? Four parcels of fairly expensive land seems like a pretty big tip." I took a sip of coffee.

Monique went from red to white in about two seconds. For a moment, I thought she might faint. She grabbed the edge of the table and swayed. "What do you know about the land?"

"I know your name is on at least four parcels that Alan was able to snap up cheap after the King Snake

Fire." Four parcels that were currently housing marijuana operations.

"And?" Her hand holding the coffeepot trembled a little.

"I know he put your name on all the deeds. Why is that, Monique? Did he owe you something?" I asked.

She shook her head. "No. It wasn't like that at all." She looked around. "I can't really talk here or now. I get off at one thirty. I'll explain everything. Or at least everything I know."

"Deal. Come to the funeral home. We can talk there," I said.

She took a step back. "Are you kidding? No way. That place gives me the creeps."

"You know you're talking about my home, right?" It still bugged me that people saw us that way.

She shrugged. "If the house fits, Death Ray."

I ate my oatmeal and paid with exact change. That Death Ray dig cost her a tip.

Chapter Twenty-Four

We ended up deciding to meet at the gazebo at two. I waited for Monique in the shade of a live oak tree. The heat wasn't too bad. Or I was getting used to it again. There was a light breeze that felt a bit like a low-powered blow dryer running over my whole body, but it also rustled the leaves enough to create shadow patterns that danced across the cracked cement around the stage and across the benches surrounding it. Around the edges of the square, setup was already starting for the Fire Festival. Booths were getting set up and hay bales were being strategically placed as seating. I was there five minutes early. Monique was five minutes late. Five minutes that I spent wondering if I'd spooked her and she'd run off rather than get entangled in Alan's murder investigation—what there was of it—but she walked up and sat down on the bench next to me at exactly five minutes after two.

"I didn't know anything about the properties until Alan died," she said without preamble.

I shook my head as if I had something in my ears. "What?"

She blew out a breath. "I know it sounds ridiculous, but he didn't tell me."

"How did you find out?" I asked. And what had happened to Monique's habit of making everything sound like a question?

"These envelopes used to come to my apartment, and he always told me not to open them, to leave them for him. So I did. Then after he . . . he died . . ." She hiccupped a little and pressed her fingertips to her eyes.

"Take your time," I said. Could she have really cared about Alan?

She nodded and took a few deep breaths. "After he died, I decided to look in the envelopes. You know, to check if there was something that needed dealing with. A bill to be paid or something."

"And what were they?" I asked.

"Utility bills. Tax statements. Bank statements. All addressed to me at my apartment, but all for those properties you were talking about." She tipped her head back to look at the sky or maybe to keep her mascara from running. Her eyes were pretty moist.

It still didn't quite make sense. If he was leasing those properties to Professor Moonbeam, why was he footing the bills? Marijuana operations can suck up a lot of electricity and a lot of water. So Alan was that forward-thinking investor that Moonbeam had mentioned. "So Alan was paying the bills for those properties?"

She nodded. "I was curious, so I went to the addresses to see what was going on."

I knew what she'd found, but I figured I'd make her say it. I sat and let the silence stretch between us.

"They're all marijuana grows. All the properties were burned during the King Snake Fire. Alan must have bought them up at a good price, and now he's letting Professor Moonbeam grow his plants on them. Alan paid for the utilities and water and then got a cut of the business on the back end too." She glanced at me as if I was going to judge her, then something hit her. "Was. He was letting Moonbeam grow there."

That part made a certain amount of sense. Moonbeam wouldn't need much besides power and water to get started. He wouldn't need a usable home or anything like that. "How did he manage to push all that paper with your name on it without you knowing about it?"

She shrugged. "He was the manager of a bank. He could do a lot of things." Her eyes welled up again. "He did a lot of things really well."

"So you two were involved," I said, stating the obvious.

She nodded. "It started off so innocent. We didn't mean for it to happen."

Monique might not have, but I had my doubts about Alan. Players gonna play. Alan had left a string of honey blondes behind him.

"He'd always sit in my section at the café when he came in for lunch. He liked that table by the window that looks out on the street."

"Mm-hmm." I'm sure the passersby weren't the only things he liked to look at. I'd bet Monique's perky butt was on the viewing menu too.

"I mentioned something about my classes at the community college, and he would always ask me how things were going. Then when I was having a real bad time with statistics, he offered to help me with my homework." She sniffled.

Oh, dear Lord. Had he seriously been recycling lines from high school?

"He was so sweet and always so interested in how I was doing and how he could help." She sighed. "I fell for him. I fell for him hard."

"You knew he was married, though, right?" I wasn't sure how observant she was, but a wife was hard to miss.

She bit her lip. "I know. It's not good to mess with another woman's man, but his marriage to Rosemarie was over already anyway."

"Did Rosemarie know that?" I asked.

She turned to look at me. "He said she did, that it was just a matter of time. They had grown apart." Her tone was wistful.

"And he said he was going to leave her for you?" Isn't that what every cheater said?

She nodded. "He said he just needed to make sure everything was in order before he did. He asked me to sign some papers. I did. It didn't seem like that much to do."

He'd do everything like buying property in his mistress's name without her even knowing about it.

A single tear overflowed from Monique's left eye and slid down her cheek, leaving a little mascara trail. "I didn't actually believe he'd do it, you know? I didn't really think he'd leave her. When I opened those envelopes and saw the bank accounts in my name and all the money . . . it hit me so hard. He really loved me. He was really going to leave Rosemarie. Why else would he have done that?"

Why else indeed? One reason I could think of was that he was funneling money into something that Rosemarie would be hard pressed to find once the divorce proceedings started.

"So what are you going to do?" I asked.

She looked up, a crease furrowing her porcelain brow. "About what?"

"About the properties and the money." What could she do? Turn them over to Rosemarie?

She looked surprised that I'd asked. "I'm going to take over where Alan left off."

My eyes widened. Monique the drug kingpin? It didn't sound right. "What do you know about running a marijuana business?"

"First of all, I'm not really running the business. I'm a landowner leasing property to someone. Second, I know plenty. I'm graduating at the end of next semester with my AA in business from Pluma Vista Community College." She sat up very straight. I'd clearly insulted her.

"Sorry, I didn't realize." I held up my hands in front of me.

She nodded. "Well, it's really helped in sorting things out."

"What needed to be sorted?" I asked.

"Oh, you know, what revenue came from where and that kind of stuff." She stopped, suddenly becoming wary. "Why do you want to know all this anyway?"

I hesitated. "I don't think Kyle Hansen killed Alan."

She sat back on the bench. "Who do you think did it?"

"I don't know. That's why when I stumbled across the properties he'd put in your name, I wanted to understand why." I leaned in. "Is there anyone in that business who would want to hurt Alan?"

"No! Of course not."

"What about Professor Moonbeam? Could there have been a falling out between them? He has a history of expressing his anger physically." I pressed.

She shook her head. "No. They had a good relationship. There weren't any problems between them." She looked at her watch. "Look, I have to go. I have Econ at three o'clock, and the professor gives the death stare to anyone who walks in late." She stood up.

"Thank you for explaining this all to me," I said. "Monique, who else knew about you and Alan?"

"Nobody," she said with great emphasis.

I shot her a look. "Nobody? Someone knows. This town runs on gossip. I can't fart on Main Street without it ending up on the front page of the *Free Press*."

Monique snorted. "That doesn't have anything to do with gossip. That's because that Rafe guy has a crush on you."

"What? No. He just wants to use me as a source." I waved the information away.

"He sure wants to use you for something. I don't think it's as a source, though," she said. "Does the information about Alan and me have to go any further? Can it stay between us?" She smiled at me.

She was really cute. "I don't think you're going to be able to keep it between us, Monique. People are going to notice, especially if you keep buying Louboutins." I stopped for a second. "Is that a Birkin bag?"

She clutched the purse to her chest. "There was a lot of money in those accounts. I thought it would be okay to buy myself a few things."

A few really nice and really expensive things. "Someone besides me is going to notice."

"Yeah, but they won't know where the money came from. Alan's name isn't on anything. Keep it between us?" She looked hopeful.

Birkin bags weren't something you bought off the rack. I tried to calculate how long it had been since Alan had died and Monique said she'd opened those envelopes. "Monique, are you one hundred percent sure you didn't dip into that money before Alan died? Maybe just the tiniest bit?"

She turned even redder. "Okay. I did. I peeked into some envelopes, and there was so much money! I just wanted a few nice things. Then Alan noticed, and he got so mad at me. That's why I was working all those extra shifts. I was trying to earn some money to put back into the accounts."

It was going to take a hell of a lot of extra shifts to get enough tips for a Birkin bag. "And now?"

She shrugged. "Well, it's all my money now, isn't it? It seems kind of silly for me to break my neck to pay myself back."

"Doesn't some of that money belong to Professor Moonbeam?" I asked.

"Some of it. Not all of it. He'll get his when the time comes." She hesitated. "I haven't explained it to my folks yet, and I'm not sure how my dad is going to take it. You're not going to tell, are you?"

I considered what it would feel like to tell my father I was a married man's mistress and had come into money and property because he'd died unexpectedly while trying to hide money from his current wife in my name. "I can see that. I certainly won't spread it around." It would get around anyway, though.

"Thanks!" she said and nearly skipped off to her car parked in a shady spot at the back of the parking lot. She hadn't upgraded the car. Yet. It was a blue Honda Civic with a yellow front panel. I wondered how long she'd keep that around.

She got in, turned the key, and then the car exploded.

Chapter Twenty-Five

The Verbena Free Press

WEDNESDAY, JULY 24

Waitress Saved by Assistant Funeral Director

A Honda Civic owned by popular Cold Clutch Canyon Café waitress Monique Woodall exploded in the Civic Center parking lot on Tuesday. Desiree Turner, assistant funeral director at the Turner Family Funeral Home, was in the area on unspecified business and saw the explosion. With no thought to her own safety, Ms. Turner ran to the vehicle and saw that the front had not been affected by the explosion. She was able to pull Ms. Woodall from the vehicle before flames from the back of the car enveloped the entire front seat.

Ms. Woodall is in stable condition at Verbena Memorial Hospital having suffered only minor burns. Doctors say she will likely be released later in the day.

Ms. Turner suffered burns to her hands but was otherwise unharmed.

Luke Butler sat across from me in the interview room with his arms crossed over his chest. He'd been waiting in the hospital parking lot for me to be released. He'd opened the door of his squad car and said, "We need to talk."

We did. I'd kind of hoped to wait until I could get home to wash the smoke smell out of my hair and put on something that wasn't mildly singed, but I've had all kinds of dreams that never came true.

"Lay it out for me, Desiree," he said.

I stared at him.

"What?" he asked.

"You called me Desiree."

"You told me to stop calling you Death Ray."

"I had no idea that would be all it would take to get you to do that. All I had to do was ask?" I'd have done that in fourth grade if I'd known that was all it took.

He shrugged. "Is this really what you want to focus on right now?"

I shook my head. "No. You're right. We have much more important things to discuss. I'm pretty sure I figured out who actually killed Alan Brewer."

"Me too. Kyle Hansen. It was his gun. He had motive. He had opportunity." Luke ticked his points off on his fingers.

"He's a lousy shot and faints at the sight of blood and is one of the sweetest men I've ever met." I would have ticked off my points on my fingers, but my hands were too bandaged up.

"So?" Luke rocked his chair onto its back legs.

"Don't you even want to hear who I'm pretty sure did it?" I rocked my chair back too. Just to show him I could.

He made a move-along gesture. "Fine. Lay it on me."

"Professor Moonbeam." I thumped my chair down and watched his reaction. I was not disappointed. He'd been itching to have a reason to go after Moonbeam, and now I was giving him something to scratch.

Luke brought the front legs of his chair down with a thump too. "Why would Professor Moonbeam shoot Alan Brewer?"

"I don't know all the specifics, but I think they argued over money." Maybe Alan was siphoning too much off the top or double-crossing Moonbeam in some other way. I was pretty certain a halfway decent forensic accountant could figure it out. More likely, Moonbeam noticed the money Monique had taken out of the account and thought he'd been double-crossed, and that had started the whole mess.

"Wait. Why would Alan and Moonbeam have any kind of money thing to argue over?" Luke asked.

Here's where I knew I would get a really great reaction. "Because they were partners in Moonbeam's marijuana business."

Luke snorted. "Right, Death Ray. The local bank president got himself all tied up in the drug business."

"I'm back to being Death Ray?" That was disappointing at the very least. I thought giving him Moonbeam on a platter would entitle me to permanent Desiree status.

"Fine. Explain this to me." He crossed his arms over his chest.

"Okay. You might want to take notes." I laid it all out for him. I told him how Alan had bought properties on the cheap after the King Snake Fire and put them in Monique's name and had then laundered the money through the Clean Green Car Wash.

Halfway through my explanation, he got up and grabbed a notepad and a pen and made me start over at the beginning. I finally reached the end of my theory. "Monique? What does Monique have to do with it?" Luke shook his head like a cartoon dog.

I waited for him to figure it out. He didn't. "She and Alan were . . . special friends."

"Ohhhh," he said. Then he made a face. "He's, like, old enough to be her dad."

"And that's so unusual." I rolled my eyes. "He's nearly old enough to be Rosemarie's dad too." He was probably older than Christine too.

"Point taken. So why would they have been fighting over money? Was Alan ripping him off?" He sighed. "Alan was kind of a slimy bastard. I wouldn't be surprised."

"I don't know for sure, but I don't think he was." This was where I ended up on some shaky ground. "I think Moonbeam *thought* Alan was ripping him off."

"Why?"

"Monique figured out there were bank accounts in her name and made some purchases. Birkin bags don't come cheap." The girl had taste. You had to give her that.

"Birkin what?"

"It's a purse. A really expensive purse. There were also the Louboutin shoes she wore at the funeral." Luke would be able to figure it out for sure. He'd be able to get access to those bank accounts with a court order. That would make everything clearer. I wasn't sure it really mattered, though.

"Shoes and a purse? How much could that cost?" He waved away the suggestion.

"Depending on her taste, around ten thousand dollars. Enough that someone might notice money coming out of an account." I leaned forward.

He looked horrified. "Who carries a ten-thousand-dollar purse?"

"At the moment, Monique Woodall," I said. "So suppose Moonbeam confronts Alan about the missing money. Alan denies any knowledge or says it's nothing. Moonbeam gets mad. You know he gets really mad, right?

Like the kind of mad that lands you in court-mandated anger management classes."

Luke nodded. "I'd heard."

"He steals Kyle's gun, shoots Alan, bada bing, bada boom." I dusted my hands together as well as I could through the bandages.

"How does he know anything about Kyle's gun?" Luke asked, eyes narrowed.

"He was at Lola and Kyle's house for the big garden tour. He could have seen it then." It all fit together perfectly.

Luke blinked. "Why frame Kyle?"

"Why not frame Kyle? He's handy. Thanks to Rafe, everybody knew about the fight between Lola and Rosemarie and about the emu." Everyone knew that Lola and Kyle had a motive to get rid of their neighbors. Seemingly half the town knew they had a gun and where they kept it.

"So Kyle was the perfect fall guy." Luke stood up. "Thank you, Desiree. I told you this marijuana business was bad news. I told you somebody was gonna get shot."

"As much as it pains me to say this, Luke, you were right."

We were almost to the door when he stopped. "So why try to get rid of Monique?" he asked.

"Maybe he didn't want to share the profits? Maybe she was interfering? I'm not sure. I do think that once you get away with killing someone, it probably seems like it could be a good solution to a lot of your problems."

*   *   *

Luke gave me a ride home. I took a shower, put on clean clothes, rebandaged my hands, and went into the kitchen to get some non-Jell-O food substances. Hospital food seriously sucks.

Donna was already in the kitchen, sitting in one chair with her feet up on another. Greg was at the stove stirring something that smelled really good. "What are you making?"

He turned and smiled at me. "Mac and cheese. Don't worry. Donna's supervising so I make it right."

I clutched my chest. "For me?" Mac and cheese was my favorite, my go-to comfort food.

"We figured you deserved it after pulling people from burning cars," Donna said.

I sat down across from her. "Will there be pie for dessert?"

She smiled. "Janet Provost brought a strawberry rhubarb one over this morning."

I squinted at her. "Tell me the truth. Am I really dead? Have I gone to heaven?"

"No. And I am a professional when it comes to knowing whether or not people are dead," she assured me. "Oh, Tanya Medina dropped off something for you too."

I clapped my hands and then really wished I hadn't. "It's a painting. It's so beautiful."

"Why did you want a painting?" she asked.

"For my room. It needed a little something."

"I'll hang it for you after lunch," Greg said, setting a bowl in front of me and one in front of Donna. "For now, maybe take a minute and relax."

It was good advice. I decided to take it.

Chapter Twenty-Six

The Verbena Free Press

THURSDAY, JULY 25

Local Marijuana Grower Arrested for Murder

Professor Moonbeam, owner of Professor Moonbeam's Dispensary and Bakery, was arrested for the murder of Alan Brewer. Sources have revealed that Brewer, president of the Verbena Union Bank, and Moonbeam were involved in a complicated scheme to launder the money from Moonbeam's marijuana business.

According to authorities, Moonbeam became suspicious that Brewer was siphoning funds out of the business, and when he saw an opportunity to remove Brewer and lay the blame on Brewer's neighbor, Kyle Hansen, he took it. Hansen and his wife, Lola, had been involved in an ongoing dispute with Brewer's wife, Rosemarie, that began with the death of an emu. All charges against Kyle Hansen have been dropped.

It's possible that Professor Moonbeam might also be responsible for the explosive device planted in the Honda Civic belonging to Monique Woodall of Verbena. Ms. Woodall was rescued from her vehicle by Desiree Turner, assistant funeral director at Turner Family Funeral Home.

Professor Moonbeam has claimed that he is innocent of all charges.

Uncle Joey walked after me carrying a box. "Are you sure you should be doing this, Desiree? I can handle it."

I consulted the map we'd been given to show us where our booth was. "It's a two-person job. You know that, and I'm fine."

He shook his head. "I don't like it, Desiree. I don't like any of this."

"You've made that clear." After the delicious mac and cheese, which Greg had made precisely right, and the lovely pie from Janet, my family had sat me down and had a long discussion about what I should and should not be doing. The "should not" list included investigating murders and pulling people from burning cars.

We found our spot. Uncle Joey set down the box he was carrying and went back to the car to get another. I started unpacking our ringtoss supplies. It was hot, and I started to regret insisting on helping out as I felt the sweat begin to trickle down my back. I could have easily played the invalid card for another day or so.

"Hey, hero!" Jasmine said as she sauntered up while I unpacked. "What are you doing?"

"I'm setting up for the Fire Festival." I turned to face her as I answered. "Duh."

She jumped back. "Girl, what happened to your eyebrows?"

I sighed. "Singed off when I pulled Monique out of her car. I tried to draw them back in. I take it I didn't do a great job."

Jasmine cocked her head to one side. "They lack a little symmetry."

I held up my bandaged hands. "It's kind of hard to do much with these all wrapped up."

"Honestly, they kind of go with the black eye." She made a circle gesture in the air. "It's like a whole gestalt you've got going on. You might even set a trend."

"Thanks," I said. "I feel so much better now. Where's your booth?"

She frowned. "Way in the back. I don't know if I'll get any foot traffic at all."

"I can't believe you decided to be a fortune-teller."

"After I said that to you, I realized how perfect it would be for me. Everyone has the same fortune at my booth. If you work through your problems, you'll find happiness and contentment. Easy peasy." She smiled. "Hey, look who's out of the hospital." Jasmine pointed down the sidewalk to Monique, who was walking toward us with a lot of purpose and determination.

She marched up to the booth. I hadn't seen her since the ambulances had driven us off to Verbena Memorial. Her eyebrows were gone too, but she'd done a much better job than I had of drawing hers back in. Other than that, she seemed pretty unscathed. "What the hell did you do?"

"Uh, saved your life? Cleared Kyle Hansen's name? Made sure a criminal was locked up?" That might be overstating. Whoever had put the bomb in Monique's car hadn't done a terrific job. It was possible that she would have gotten out on her own.

She took a step toward me, crowding into my space. "Don't get cute with me. The raid. Why the hell did you call in that raid?"

"What raid?" I asked.

"The raid of all four of my properties plus my apartment." She jabbed her finger into my chest.

"Ouch," I said, brushing her hand away. "Slow your roll. I have no idea what you're talking about."

Jasmine stepped in between us. "You better step off, Monique."

She rolled her eyes. "Or what?"

Jasmine crossed her arms over her chest. "You don't want to know."

"What I want to know is who else would know to call in a federal task force at all my properties and at my apartment? It certainly wasn't in Moonbeam's interest." She kicked at our booth.

"How could they raid you? I thought you were a legal grow. Didn't Alan fill out all the paperwork? Or Moonbeam?" I sat down on the chair inside the booth, feeling suddenly exhausted.

"Of course all the paperwork was filled out! Alan and Professor Moonbeam took care of all that ages ago. These are not amateurs I'm dealing with. During the raid, we even had someone from the county get on the phone with one of the deputies." She threw her hands in the air and stepped back away. Jasmine relaxed her stance.

None of this sounded right. None of this made sense. "What did the deputy do?" I asked.

"He laughed and hung up the phone. He didn't care. He said because they were a federal task force, it didn't matter that we were legal with the county and the state." She kicked the booth again. "They destroyed the crops. They took everything."

"Monique, I'm so sorry, but I had nothing to do with this. You have to know that whoever did call in that raid must have done it days ago. I didn't know about everything in time to make that happen." Someone had though. Someone had been unhappy enough about those grows to figure out how to get them shut down. That wasn't easy. It would have taken time and planning.

Monique started to calm down. "Desiree, they put me in handcuffs. Handcuffs! I thought I was going to be arrested and taken to jail. Strip-searched and deloused. All those awful things." A little sob escaped from her.

It must have been terrifying. "But they didn't arrest you. Did they arrest anyone else? Anyone at all?"

"Well, Moonbeam. But that wasn't for the mari-juana." She shook her head. "No. They ended up letting us all go, but not before they destroyed everything. It's a mess. They destroyed the whole crop."

"What will you do?" I asked.

She sighed. "Shut down, I suppose. I hate to do it. If Alan thought it was a good investment, it must have been one. I don't see how we can come back from this though, especially without Moonbeam. He was the one who knew the plants."

I wasn't sure if Alan thought it was a good investment or a good place to hide money from Rosemarie before he extricated himself from that particular union.

"I miss him, you know." She traced a design on the counter of our booth.

"Moonbeam?" I asked.

"No! Alan." She looked away for a second, but not before I saw her eyes glisten. "It's especially hard because I can't really talk about it to anyone. Right now, you're the only one who knows about us." She looked over at Jasmine, who mimed locking her lips with a key and throwing it away.

I reached across and patted her arm. "It's extrahard to have a loss and not be able to process it with anyone."

She wiped at her cheeks with her sleeve. "I wish I'd known that the last time we were together would be the last time I'd ever see him. I would have . . ." Her words trailed off.

"Would have what?" I asked.

"I don't know." She picked at the edge of the booth with her fingernail. "I always tried to make sure he knew how much I loved him when he walked out the door. I guess that's going to have to be enough. He was a little mad at me that last time though."

"Why?"

She smiled a little. "Well, the money. Plus, I guess I got a little carried away with making sure he knew I loved him. We'd been together all afternoon. He knew Rosemarie was going to Miss Delia's funeral and that she wouldn't call him or anything for an hour or so."

So while Rosemarie and Lola were rolling around on the floor of the Turner Family Funeral Home, Alan had been rolling around with Monique.

"After we were . . . done"—she blushed—"he turned his phone on, and it went wild with messages. I guess they must have been from her over at the police station. He got dressed and rushed out the door. He didn't even take a shower or kiss me good-bye. He probably didn't even know I'd sort of left a little love bite on his chest."

"Oh! The hickey! That was from you?" And I'd thought it was from Rosemarie.

She turned an even deeper shade of red. "I didn't mean to. I just got carried away." She blew out a breath. "Look, I'm sorry I accused you of calling in that raid. Not many people know what's happening on those properties and how they're linked. You're one of them. I guess I leapt to a conclusion."

"Yeah. Never assume," I said, but I was starting to go through the mental list of who might have known to call in that raid and who would have wanted to. My list was at zero.

She rolled her eyes. "My dad says that all the time. It makes an *ass* out of *u* and *me*."

"Dads aren't all bad," I said. This would be my first Fire Festival without Dad. I used to come back for it all the time. He was great at the booth, calling out at people like a carnival barker.

"Yeah," she said. "Sorry about yours."

She walked away. I turned to Jasmine. "What exactly were you going to do?"

She shrugged. "I'm not sure. I'm glad we didn't have to find out."

Uncle Joey walked back up. "What was that about?" he asked, dropping another box on the counter.

I shook my head. "I'm not really sure."

Chapter Twenty-Seven

The Verbena Free Press

FRIDAY, JULY 24

Local Marijuana Grow Raided

Four properties plus the apartment of a local landowner were raided by a federal drug task force from Norte Costa County. Despite the fact that the grower had all proper paperwork in place for Pluma Vista County, the task force had obtained a warrant. All the plants have been confiscated.

A representative from the task force claimed that they had received an anonymous tip approximately one week before the raid giving details on the location and ownership of the properties.

The day of the Fire Festival had finally arrived. I helped Uncle Joey get the last of our booth set up, bought two serrano sangrias—they'd grown on me—and carried them over to Jasmine's booth. She was right.

She was way in the back. It was hard to even see her booth. You had to go around a corner to find it.

I handed her the drink. "So who did you piss off to get such a bad placement?"

"I'm honestly not sure. Someone's mad, though." She took a sip of her drink, then tied a scarf around her head as we stood in line. "How do I look?"

I smiled. "Like Rihanna when she was on *Saturday Night Live*."

She smiled back. "Nice!"

"Yeah, nice," a voice said behind us.

We both turned. It was one of the men from Jasmine's anger management class, the one that had seemed familiar. Where had I seen him? He took two more steps toward us. It was his walk. Where had I seen that gait before?

It hit me like a hammer to the forehead. The shadow that had crept out from a doorway as we'd driven down the street. The legs that I'd seen on the security camera footage from the Civic Center parking lot.

Jasmine stiffened. "Walter, what are you doing here?"

"Just stopping by. Wanted to say hello." He kicked at the ground for a second. "Don't you have anything you want to say to me?"

"Anything I have to say to you I'll say in my office during our regularly scheduled meetings," Jasmine said. Her voice was much too calm. Something was definitely wrong.

I looked around. No one else was nearby. I wondered if I should make a run for it and get help.

"I thought you might want to say thank you," Walter said.

"For what?" Jasmine asked.

"You know. The chocolates. The lightbulbs. Dragging in your garbage cans. The money for the drinks you like so much." He gestured at the cup in her hand.

"That was you?" Jasmine asked.

He took another step toward her. I took one back, but Jasmine didn't. I hoped she had a better idea of what she was doing than she did during our face-off with Monique. Walter looked considerably more scary. "Of course it was me. Who did you think it was? You knew. I saw the way you looked at me in group. Giving me those special smiles. Then you pretend you don't know me in public." He shook his head. "It's not right, Jasmine. A man deserves respect."

"Walter, I explained to you at our first meeting that I wouldn't acknowledge you in public unless you spoke to me first. It's for your privacy." Jasmine sounded weary, as if she'd given the same explanation dozens of times. "No one is disrespecting you."

"Right." He took another step toward us, and his hand came out from behind his back. He had a knife. "No one disrespects me and gets away with it."

I wanted to scream, but I think the only noise that came out was more like a squeak. Then I saw movement over Walter's shoulder. Officer Haynes. I was about to say something, but she held her finger to her lips. She stepped quietly across the grass toward us.

"Walter, you need to put that knife down and leave," Jasmine said. I didn't know if she'd seen Haynes yet. Her gaze seemed to stay on Walter's face, not even wavering down to the knife.

"Not until you say thank you." The hand with the knife rose.

Haynes leapt forward, grabbing Walter's wrist. She twisted it. Walter screamed and the knife fell from his grasp. He whirled around. He had to be at least six inches taller than the officer and easily outweighed her by eighty pounds or so. He wrenched away and pulled his fist back. He was going to slam it right into her jaw. She was faster, though. As his fist pummeled toward her, she grabbed it, ducked beneath it, and twisted again. Within seconds, he was on the ground. It took her only a moment to handcuff him, then with her knee in his back, she touched the buttons on the radio strapped to her shoulder. "Officer requires assistance. Back corner. Therapy booth."

I let out a whoosh of breath I hadn't realized I was holding.

Jasmine stood like a statue, not moving.

"Jaz, are you okay?" I tapped her shoulder. She didn't move. "Jaz?"

Finally, she blinked. "Walter was my stalker," she said. She shook her head. "I should have known. It's totally consistent with his diagnosis. I should have seen all the signs of transference. Thank you, Carlotta."

I looked at Jasmine and back to the person I thought of as Officer Haynes, but apparently Jasmine thought of as Carlotta. "You know each other?"

Jaz blushed a tiny bit. "We've met."

Carlotta turned to me. "We more than met. We went out then . . . some things got in the way, and she wouldn't take my calls anymore."

I looked at Officer Haynes. We were a little off the beaten path that most of the cops walked during the festival. "Did you just happen to be here at just the right time to deal with this guy?"

She blushed and turned to Jasmine. "Not exactly. Look. I wanted to figure out how I could get you to go out with me again so I was sort of maybe stalking you a little. You know, driving by your house and your office. Trying to get a sense of your schedule and what you like."

"Wait," I said. "I thought Walter was the stalker."

"He was. So when I was sort of stalking Jasmine, I saw him doing all kinds of creepy things up on your porch and in your side yard. Nothing he'd done was technically illegal." She pressed her knee a little harder into Walter's back and he grunted. "But I knew you were in real trouble."

"Why didn't you tell me?" Jasmine asked.

"At first, I didn't tell you because then I would have to admit that I'd found out you had a stalker when I was stalking you. Then I did decide to tell you, and I called you. Did you happen to notice the ten or twelve messages I left you that you didn't answer?" Carlotta's eyebrows went up.

Jasmine blushed. "I didn't even listen to them. I figured you were just asking me out again."

Carlotta shrugged. "There you go."

"But you kept an eye on her, didn't you?" I said. It had always been Carlotta driving by in the squad car every time we'd seen Walter, and those were only the times we know about.

She shrugged. "Protect and serve."

Two other officers came running up, and Carlotta stood. "Take him in." She pointed to the knife. "Book him for assault."

They cleared out, but Jasmine still hadn't really moved. She stared at Carlotta. I took that as my cue and slipped out of the booth. I figured they had it from there, and Uncle Joey would be needing me at our booth.

Everything was buzzing around the gazebo. The sun was starting to set, and the Delta breezes were starting to pick up, carrying the scent of the bananas Foster being served at the Cold Clutch Canyon Café booth. Uncle Joey had set up the ringtoss, and we had a fairly steady stream of kids wearing foam flame hats in red and orange and pink coming through, trying their luck, and pretty much all leaving with a little stuffed animal. Uncle Joey kept the line moving and retrieved the rings. I handed out rings and prizes. It was a good division of labor.

Rafe sauntered up, notepad in hand. "A ringtoss?"

I sighed. "I know. Not very original, but it's tried and true. The kids like it." I gestured at the line.

"And what's with the stuffed dogs? Everybody else's stuff is pretty thematic. The bank is giving out tissues that look like money. The computer place is giving out those stress balls." He paused to snap a picture of a particularly cute kid tossing a ring. The kid missed, but I handed him a little stuffed dog anyway. "Shouldn't they be little skeletons or crows or something?"

"Nobody wants their kids to have funeral-themed stuffed animals. It's morbid." I sipped at my second serrano sangria from the Tappiano's booth.

"Isn't everything associated with funeral homes kind of morbid?" He stepped back and snapped a picture of me.

I threw my still-bandaged hands in front of my singed and bruised face. "We've been over this. I'm not news," I said. "Plus, I'm not exactly photo ready, what with the black eye and the lack of eyebrows."

"I beg to differ." He grinned.

Which was when Nate strode up. How did he always show up when Rafe was around? Maybe I had a stalker too. "Hi, Desiree. Need any help?" He gestured at the booth but did not say hello to Rafe. Rafe didn't say hello to him either.

"No thanks. I think we've got it covered." I handed a set of rings to the next cherub and watched as she missed with each one. Then I handed her a little stuffed dog. She skipped away, happy.

Rafe looked back and forth between us and then said, "I'll be on my way, then."

Nate watched him go and then turned to me. "What is it with that guy?" he asked.

"What do you mean?"

"He's always hanging around you." He kicked a little at the ground. "He's always writing about you."

I crossed my arms over my chest. "If he is, what is it to you?"

"It's just . . ." His words trailed off.

"Just what?" I pulled some more stuffed animals from the box under the table. We were going through them pretty fast. Maybe I should start only giving them to kids who actually managed to get a ring on a post. Nah, that seemed harsh. I'd rather shut down early than send a kid away without a prize.

"Well, seeing you again has made me wonder . . ." Nate let his words drift off again.

"Wonder what?" I asked, starting to feel impatient.

"Well, we're both home again, living in the same place and . . ." A blush was spreading across his cheeks.

I couldn't believe what I was hearing. "Nate Johar, you shook hands with me."

He blinked. "What do you mean?"

"Hey, lady!" the next kid in line said.

I shoved the rings at him. "Here." Then I turned back to Nate. "The first time we saw each other again, when we said good-bye, you shook my hand." I glared at him, hands on my hips. Unbelievable. After ten years, a guy shakes your hand, and he suddenly feels he has romantic claims on you? "I haven't seen you once since we broke up freshman year."

"The timing's always been bad," he protested. "We were never here at the same time."

"That's your excuse? Bad timing? What about the handshake?" The wine might have been loosening my tongue a bit. Or numbing it with the serrano peppers. I was fairly certain I wasn't slurring, but only just.

"I don't understand." He honestly looked confused.

"If you wanted this to be something, a handshake wasn't the way to go." I remember how deflated I'd felt as he walked away.

"What should I have done?"

"Forget it." I lifted the section of the booth that would let me out. "Uncle Joey, I'm going to walk around for a bit."

He waved to me. "Have fun, and be careful with that sangria. It's stronger than you think."

I marched away, Nate at my heels. "Wait. Desiree, what should I have done?"

I whirled on him, my head spinning a little. It was possible that Uncle Joey was right and the sangria was a little stronger than I'd realized. "You should have kissed me, you idiot."

With that, he stepped forward, grabbed me by the waist, pulled me to him, and planted a long, slow, deep kiss right on my lips. I heard applause around us and at least one wolf whistle. He released me and said, "Like that?"

I tried to catch my breath. "Something like that."

"Can we go someplace to talk?" he asked.

I looked around. The square was packed with people. "There are some benches by the Civic Center. Let's go sit there."

We walked together to the next block and turned to sit on some benches tucked back into the shade of some wisteria. The second we sat, he was kissing me again. In the distance, the high school marching band began playing "Light My Fire."

I put my hands against his chest and pushed him back. "I thought we were going to talk."

"Oh," he said. "I thought that was a euphemism. You know, kind of like how we were going to study when we were in high school."

"Very funny." I punched his shoulder lightly then winced because it hurt my hands.

"Fine," he said. "What do you want to talk about?"

A movement caught my eye as someone went into the Civic Center. It was Rosemarie, carrying a bundle beneath her arm. What was she doing in the Civic Center? There was nothing going on in there tonight. In fact, it should have been locked up. Maybe she still had the key from the reception she'd held there.

A few seconds later, Monique walked up and went in the same door. I sat up straight. "That's not good," I said.

"What?" Nate asked.

"Rosemarie and Monique together in the Civic Center." A horrible thought dawned on me. Maybe I'd been wrong about Professor Moonbeam. He'd said he was innocent, but Jasmine was right. Everyone said that. What if he really wasn't though? If I had figured out that Alan and Monique were having an affair, couldn't someone else have figured it out too? What if that someone was his wife? His wife who had had an affair with him when he was married to someone else, who would know the signs, who might have seen that big old love bite on his chest and figured out where he'd been when he wasn't bailing her out of jail for getting in a fistfight at an old lady's funeral. His wife who had been working hard at getting into his computer and who might then have figured out his connection to the marijuana trade and might have called in a raid. The consensus was that it had to have been someone who was pissed off to call in a raid on a legal grow. Who would be more pissed off about the situation that a wife who was being cheated on physically and financially?

What had Luke said at the very beginning? That it was almost always the spouse? But then afterward he'd said she was too grief stricken. Then I remembered what Olive had said to me about Maddie Ledbetter. Sometimes grief and guilt look an awful lot alike. Maybe all this time Rosemarie had been struggling with her guilt and not her grief at all. No wonder she didn't want anyone to come stay with her. She couldn't tell anyone what she'd done. She's the one who must have tried to kill Monique with a car bomb too. Moonbeam had no reason to do that. Rosemarie did, though.

I stood, wobbling a little on my feet. I was in no shape to go chasing around looking for help. "I don't have time to explain. Go get someone. Luke or Carlotta or, well, anybody. Tell them to come fast, or there might be another murder in Verbena."

"What are you going to do?" Nate asked.

"I'll call for help." I pulled out my phone.

"Promise?" he asked.

I nodded, and he took off at a run.

I dialed Luke's cell phone number as best I could with my bandaged hands. It went straight to voice mail. Next I tried Jasmine. Maybe she was still with Officer Haynes.

Voice mail again. The damn band. They must be playing so loud that no one could hear their phones ring.

Then I heard the scream. There wasn't time to wait for help. I ran to the door of the Civic Center and slammed through. The air-conditioned chill hit my skin and I shivered. The lights in the hallway were off, leaving everything shadowed and dark. Which way had they gone? I listened and heard a noise from the main hall. I rushed through the door.

Monique was cowering in the corner. Rosemarie had a bundle in one hand and a lighter in the other. I could smell the gasoline from the doorway.

"Look out!" Monique yelled. "She's going to set us on fire!"

Rosemarie turned and glared at me. "What is it with you? You're always in the way. Get over there next to Monique."

I walked slowly to where Monique stood. "What are you going to do?"

"It's going to look like an accident. A spark from one of the fire dancers or a candle left to burn too long or an errant firework or the rewiring wasn't done right. I'll make sure the curtains catch and then poof! Monique will be gone." She was breathing hard. Her eyes looked wild.

I wasn't well versed in arson investigations, but I guessed I would have to take her word for it. I didn't want to find out if she was right. I needed to keep her talking.

I had to buy enough time for Nate to bring help. "Why, Rosemarie? I really don't understand why."

"Really? I was losing everything. Everything! Vincent was dead. And Alan?" She shook her head.

"Yes." I leaned forward. "Alan."

"Do you know what time Kyle came to bail Lola out the day we had our . . . disagreement?" she asked. "Disagreement" seemed a pretty mild description of what had happened in the Magnolia Room, but I let it pass. I wanted to hear more. "Two o'clock. Lola was out of a cell and on her way home by two o'clock. Do you know what time Alan came for me?"

I remembered Monique saying that there had been a lot of messages on Alan's phone that afternoon. "Later than two o'clock, I'm guessing."

"Four o'clock!" she screamed. "Four! I called and called and called. I called his cell phone. I called the bank. No one knew where he was. He was supposed to be my person."

"Your person?" I asked.

"Yes, my person. The person who comes when I call. The person who bails me out of jail, who comes to the emergency room when I'm hurt, who has my back in a fight. My person. Lola's person came for her right away. She hadn't even had her phone call yet and Kyle was there. Where was Alan?" She made a face and turned away.

Oh, her person. Like Jasmine was my person.

"And you should have smelled him when he came home that night." She put her hand over her mouth.

"So you suspected he'd been with another woman?" I asked.

"Suspected? I knew! I'd already been suspicious." She shook her head. "I'd seen the signs: the late nights, the phone calls he'd hang up on the second I came in the room, the waxing."

I really would have rather not known about Alan waxing. "But the smell was what made you decide he was definitely cheating?"

"The smell and that big hickey on his chest. Oh, he tried to hide it. Came to bed with a T-shirt, saying he was cold. Cold? Who is ever cold in the Central Valley in the summer?" She shook her head.

"When did you decide to kill him?" I asked.

She sighed. "It wasn't really planned. Everything came together in some weird way. It was like the universe was telling me to kill him, like it was meant to be."

I was pretty sure if the universe told you something like that, you were supposed to hang up on it and call a doctor immediately. "How so?"

"Alan knew I was mad at him, so he was being all extrahelpful. He offered to go down to the chicken coop to collect the eggs for me. He hated doing that. Those eggs aren't so clean when you take them right from the coop, and he didn't like to get his hands dirty. I stood on the porch and watched him walk over the hill toward the coop. While I was standing there, I saw Kyle leave his house with the dogs. I knew he'd be gone for close to an hour. It hit me like a thunderclap. I knew where Kyle and Lola kept their gun. I knew they almost never locked their house, and if they did, they kept their spare key in that ceramic duck."

Horse, I corrected silently.

"It seemed fitting. Kyle took Vincent from me by not controlling his vicious attack dogs and never had to pay the price. I decided I'd get rid of two men I hated at once. It wouldn't bring Vincent back, but there would at least be justice for his death, and I'd get rid of Alan all with one shot." She giggled. It was a horrible sound.

"Vincent?" Monique whispered.

"My emu." She wiped at her eye. "Damn it! I loved that bird."

Monique turned to me. "How can someone love an emu?"

I shrugged. I also had wondered about the nature of Rosemarie's relationship with her emu. "The heart wants what the heart wants." I turned back to Rosemarie. "But now Monique? I mean, I know who she was to Alan, but why kill her?"

"Another one who wasn't getting punished for anything! She slept with my husband. Not once, but many times. And what happened to her? She ended up with a bunch of property and a new business. How was that fair? So I called in a raid on the marijuana grows, and now I'm going to burn her up." Rosemarie smiled. "It's going to feel so good."

She had a point. It wasn't exactly fair, but if you killed everyone who got some kind of unfair deal, the world would have a much sparser population.

"Maybe if you'd paid Alan as much attention as you'd paid that damn emu, he wouldn't have been looking for a little something-something somewhere else," Monique said, stepping forward. "How fair was it that he left his first wife just so you could snub him for some stupid faux ostrich?"

I threw her a glance. I didn't think antagonizing Rosemarie was a good way for any of us to get out of there alive.

"Faux ostrich!" Rosemarie screamed. "You little hussy!"

"Me? Well, I'm rubber and you're glue," Monique said. "How was what I did with Alan any different than what you did with Alan when he was still married to Christine?"

Rosemarie's lips tightened. "It was totally different. We were in love. We were destined to be together. You . . . you were just a distraction."

"Distracting enough that he was going to leave you." Monique jutted out a hip.

Rosemarie snarled.

The door flew open. Carlotta and Luke burst in, guns drawn. Rafe was right behind them, camera up and clicking. "Hold it right there, Rosemarie. Put that torch down!" Luke yelled.

Monique screamed. "She did it! She killed Alan!"

"We know. We heard everything." Carlotta didn't even glance at Monique. She kept her eyes trained on Rosemarie just like Jasmine had never looked away from Walter. "Come on, Rosemarie. You don't want to do this. You don't want to hurt any more people. Put the torch down."

Rosemarie's hands began to tremble. "I don't know. I don't know what to do."

"Sure you do," Officer Haynes said, her voice silky smooth. "Put the torch on the floor, and put the lighter down too."

Rosemarie looked back and forth at the wad of cloth in her hands and the lighter as if she wasn't really sure how they got there. "I didn't have any choice," she said.

"Of course not," Carlotta agreed. "What else could you have done? We all understand that. Just put the torch down."

Rosemarie began to weep, her shoulders shaking. She swiped at her nose with the back of her arm.

Monique made a noise of disgust. "Oh, for Pete's sake! Why are you sniveling? You killed him. You killed the man who loved me. I'm the one who gets to cry. Not you!"

Rosemarie's head came up, her eyes blazing with hatred. "You! You should get nothing." And with that, she flicked the lighter and touched it to the torch. It went up like a Roman candle.

Rosemarie threw the ignited torch at Monique. Somehow my old volleyball instincts kicked in. I launched myself, stretching my arms out in front of me, bandaged hands clasped together, and I bumped that torch halfway across the room. Rafe raced for it, pulled off his shirt, and smothered the fire.

Rosemarie took off toward the side door, but it wouldn't open. She pounded a few times on the door as if someone might come and let her escape the trap she'd set for Monique and then sank to the floor. Carlotta hauled her to her feet. "Rosemarie Brewer, you are under arrest for the murder of Alan Brewer and"—she looked around the room—"and probably a bunch of other stuff, but we'll start there. You have the right to remain silent . . ." They marched out of the room.

I sat down hard in one of the plastic chairs. Rafe came over and sat down next to me. "I have no idea how I'm going to write that up."

I gave him some side eye. "I'm sure you'll figure something out. I, however, have no comment."

He smiled. "It'd be easier with some help."

"What kind of help?" I asked, leaning into him. Suddenly I was terribly cold, and I could feel his warmth next to me.

He threw an arm around my shoulder. "The kind that does some articles for the paper."

"Feature stuff? Recipes? New store openings?" I made a disgusted noise in the back of my throat.

He shook his head. "No. Real stuff. I mean, you figured all this out. What else might you be able to figure out?"

Not him, apparently.

"I think this could be the start of a beautiful friendship." He pulled me a little closer.

I became all too aware of the fact that he wasn't wearing a shirt and that he looked pretty good that way.

Before I could reply, Nate and Jasmine came skidding into the room. "We just saw Carlotta leaving with Rosemarie in handcuffs. What's going on?" Jaz demanded.

Nate looked at me sitting there with Rafe's naked arm resting on my shoulder. His gaze darted back and forth between us. "You're okay then?" he asked.

"A little shaken, but okay." I looked over at Jasmine and said, "It's a long story."

Monique snorted. "No, it's not. Rosemarie tried to kill me with a torch. Desiree saved me."

Jasmine's eyebrows went up. "You're a hero again?"

"I guess it depends on how you frame it." I was exhausted—too exhausted to claim hero status. I stood up. "I think I just want to go home."

"I'll walk you," Nate said.

Rafe stood too and shrugged into the burned remnants of his shirt. "I'll get over to the newspaper and try to write this up. I want it up on the website tonight."

We all walked out of the Civic Center as Luke walked up with a big roll of crime scene tape to stretch around it. He gave me a salute as we walked away. "Nice work, Desiree."

"Thanks," I said.

We stopped at the Turner Family booth to let Uncle Joey know I was going home and walked the blocks to the funeral home in silence. When we got there, I walked back to the stairs to the family entrance. I turned to Nate. "Thanks. I think I've got it from here."

"Desiree," he said.

I held up a hand to stop him. "Whatever it is, can it wait?"

"Not really," he said. He leaned down and kissed me. Just one soft, sweet kiss. I heard a boom and looked up. The first fireworks were going off in the town square.

He grinned. "Good timing. For once."

I shook my head. "Good night."

I trudged up the stairs. There was an envelope addressed to Donna and me wedged into the doorframe. I pulled it out and opened it. There was a card inside with one word written on it: *Sorry.*

I stared at it. I knew that handwriting. I knew that quirky little way of making a *y*. It was my dad's handwriting.

I raced inside and grabbed my laptop. Donna was in the living room, sitting on the couch. I carried my laptop over to Donna. "Can you help me with this?"

"Sure. Why?" She took it from me.

I held up my bandaged hands. "Typing's not working out so well for me at the moment."

"Got it. What do you want me to do?" She flipped the computer open.

I guided her through the steps to get to the video stored from the motion-sensitive camera. She clicked it open. "You're taping our house?"

I nodded. There were a few little clips from when a bird flew up on the back porch and another one as a squirrel scampered across. Uncle Joey went in and out. Greg went in and out. I did too. Then a figure walked into view.

Donna gasped, and I sucked in some air. The person was tall and lanky. The kind of person who spent a lot of time indoors. He slid an envelope into the doorframe and then turned to walk away. When he turned, his face was in full view.

"Dad," we said in unison.

* * *

A Grave Issue

The Verbena Free Press

SUNDAY, JULY 30

Local Businesswoman Traps Murderer, Saves Day

Desiree Turner, assistant funeral director at Turner Family Funeral Home, faced off with Rosemarie Brewer, wife and alleged murderer of Alan Brewer, in the Civic Center hall during the Fire Festival this past Friday night. Ms. Turner had become suspicious of Ms. Brewer and Ms. Brewer's intentions toward Monique Woodall. She followed the two women into the Civic Center to find Ms. Brewer brandishing a gasoline-soaked torch and a lighter and threatening to burn down the Civic Center with Ms. Woodall in it.

Officer Carlotta Haynes and Detective Luke Butler of the Verbena Police Department were able to apprehend Ms. Brewer before any damage was done.

Officer Haynes said, "We do not recommend citizens taking the law into their own hands ever. The correct procedure when you suspect wrongdoing is to contact the police and let them take care of it."

Ms. Turner declined to comment on the situation.

Full Disclosure: Desiree Turner will be joining the staff of the *Verbena Free Press* as a roving reporter starting in August of this year.

Read an excerpt from

IF THE COFFIN FITS

the next

FUNERAL PARLOR MYSTERY

by LILLIAN BELL

available soon in hardcover from
Crooked Lane Books

CROOKED
LANE

NEW YORK

Chapter One

The Verbena Free Press
October 4
By Desiree Turner

Dangers of Drowsy Driving

On October 2, Verbena resident Violet Daugherty died in what police think was a drowsy driving accident. Ms. Daugherty lost control of her vehicle on County Road 202 at approximately 7:30 PM and collided with an embankment. Despite heroic efforts, doctors at the hospital were unable to bring her back to consciousness.

It's difficult to establish exact numbers when it comes to how many accidents might be caused by people falling asleep at the wheel. There's no test to be done like the ones that determine whether or not a driver has been driving under the influence. Still, estimates as to how many accidents are caused by drowsy driving go as high as 100,000 per year. Officer Carlotta Haynes of the Verbena Police

Department said, "We don't know what caused Ms. Daugherty to lose control of her car, but the lack of skid marks and the fact that no other cars were involved point to a case of drowsy driving."

We should all take steps to make sure accidents like this don't happen. If you find yourself blinking excessively, or don't remember driving the last few miles, or drift from your lane, pull over. Take a nap. Get some coffee. Walk around a bit. Nothing's important enough to risk your life and the lives of others on the road.

*   *   *

Generally, funeral directors don't see the best version of families. Sometimes we do. Sometimes there are sisters holding each other up, or a son quietly supporting a father. Sometimes hands are held and hugs are given. The burden of sorrow and the good memories of the deceased are shared. More often than not, however, there's squabbling.

Either there's been some terrible illness that has eaten away at the family's emotional, physical, spiritual, and financial resources—possibly for months or even years—or something cataclysmic has happened. A car accident. A tragic fall. An aneurysm no one knew about bursting like a malevolent Fourth of July firework in someone's brain.

People are exhausted or in shock. Neither of those states brings out the best behaviors. Daisy and Iris Fiore, however, were one of those supportive exceptions when they came in to make arrangements for their father's funeral. Daisy was the eldest by about two years. She was a little shorter and plumper with layered shoulder-length blonde hair and some well-applied makeup. Iris was one of those rail-thin women who started to look a little stringy after forty. She would be very low on the list of people to eat if our plane crashed in the Andes. Her dark hair with its gray streaks was cut in one of those sensible cuts. Sort of a reverse mullet with long bangs and short back. Neat, presentable, easy to take care of. If she was wearing makeup, it certainly didn't show. They looked so different, but their care and respect for each other was the same. Iris pulled a tissue out of her purse and handed it to Daisy when Daisy's eyes started to mist over while choosing music for the service. Daisy slipped Iris a cough drop and asked if Iris could have a glass of water when Iris got choked up picking which readings they'd like to have. They touched hands and held to each other. Which is why I was a little surprised when I heard Daisy hiss at Iris as I came back with the requested glass of water.

"What did you do?" she asked.

"Why do you always think I did something wrong?" Iris stage-whispered back.

I stopped on the other side of the door to the Lilac Room, not wanting to interrupt them. It was good to give people a little space.

"Well, did you do something wrong?" Daisy followed up. There was a tapping noise as if she was rapping something softly on the table.

There was a pause, then Iris said, "Define wrong."

Daisy made a noise of disgust. "We'll talk about this at home."

Iris replied, "There's nothing to talk about. What's done is done."

The room went silent, and I pushed through the door with the glasses of water I'd been getting from the kitchen. "Here you go," I said, acting as if I hadn't heard anything. I certainly wouldn't have even known anything could be wrong if I hadn't overheard them. They sat side by side on the plump coach, the coffee table with various brochures and forms and the ever-present box of tissues in front of them. It was a room designed to foment serenity. No bright colors. No hard edges. No bright lights.

Iris and Daisy resumed their supportive-sister act as if nothing had been said, although now it seemed kind of phony. Was this a performance they were putting on for people who were watching? Or had that moment of instant antagonism been the anomaly? I went along with the good-sister act, but I was uneasy. My role as assistant funeral director at Turner Family Funeral Home was not to stir up trouble. It was to make sure there was as little trouble as possible. My job was a lot easier if people weren't squabbling. Daisy and Iris weren't fighting, but if something was bubbling beneath the surface that could erupt at an inopportune time, I wanted to be aware of it. We went through the stack of paperwork required by law and made the other general arrangements. Nothing else tripped my sense of something being wrong.

"I doubt we'll have a very big turnout at the funeral," Daisy said, emitting a waft of honey and lemon. "Dad was sick for so long. People have forgotten they even knew him."

"I barely remember what he was like when he was well." Iris's chin trembled.

"It takes time," I said. Families often got so caught up in the care of their ill loved one that they forgot who the person was in the first place. It was part of the function of the funeral. It was a moment to go back and reflect. People dug out old photos and home movies and rediscovered who the person was, what they'd been like when they'd been healthy and whole. People shared stories that revealed who that person was and what they meant to everyone.

"You never know about attendance," I said. "If you'll fill out this form, I can get your father's obituary and an announcement of the service into the paper right away." I gestured toward that day's copy of the *Verbena Free Press* that sat on the low coffee table next to the couch. "Your father was well-known. I'm sure people will come once they know when it is."

"They sure didn't visit him in the past few years," Iris said with a sniff.

I winced. "People don't always know what to say or do. They get worried about doing the wrong thing so they don't do anything." It was a lame explanation, but it was true. People don't know how to act around death. We always want to shove it under the carpet or into a dark closet so we don't have to look at it. Then it feels unfamiliar and scary when it inevitably makes its presence known in our lives. And its presence is indeed inevitable. I grew up with death all around me. I'd thought that was normal for a very long time. It still sometimes surprised me that it isn't.

"I suppose," Iris said on a sigh. "Do we have to have the funeral right away? Could we wait a little while? So people could make arrangements to get here?"

"Of course." Since they'd already chosen to have their father embalmed, we could wait a week at least before the services.

We finished up the arrangements. As they were leaving, with Iris promising to bring by whatever clothing they wanted their father buried in and some photos for Donna to use to make the memorial video, Uncle Joey knocked on the door. Uncle Joey is my father's younger brother. He and my dad ran Turner Family Funeral Home together since before I can remember. They were always together. Best friends. Brothers. Coworkers. They took over from their father who took over from his father before him. I think everyone assumed that my sister Donna and I would take over from them some day. They were half-right for a while and now were completely right, at least for the time being. Donna did all the classes and training—she needed to do both what Uncle Joey did down in the basement and what Dad did upstairs—and took her place in the family business. I took off for Southern California when I turned eighteen without glancing in my rearview mirror, and I'd still be gone if I hadn't managed to torpedo my own career as an on-air reporter with a hot mic incident that went viral. Instead, I was back in Verbena, working at the funeral home and wondering what was next in my life.

After extending his condolences to Iris and Daisy, Uncle Joey asked, "Are you available to help me with a pick up today?"

"Sure. We're just finishing up here." I turned away from my Iris and Daisy and mouthed "who?" at Uncle Joey.

He nodded to the newspaper on the coffee table. It took me a second to get it. Violet Daugherty whose single-car accident I'd written about for the *Verbena Free Press*. I turned back toward Iris and Daisy who were exchanging their own glances between each other and also surreptitiously trying to check the time on their phones. It only took a few more minutes to finish everything up and they looked relieved to be done.

I watched them go, arm in arm, Daisy's hand tucked through Iris's elbow. When we'd had to plan the memorial service for our father, Donna and I had spent a lot of time like that. Shoulders pressed against each other as we sat on the couch. A hand placed gently on the other's hand or arm. You'd think we would have had it easier than most people. We knew the business. We knew what Dad would have wanted. We'd had months to get used to the idea that he was gone. It was entirely different when it was your own family.

Getting used to the idea that he might not actually be gone was taking even more getting used to.

I sat looking at the paperwork in front of me. Mr. Fiore had been on hospice care. His death had been expected, even, perhaps, welcomed as it released him from pain. What was it that Iris could have possibly done that would have made her sister that angry? That might or might not be wrong? And why wait until they were here at the funeral home to ask about it?

I headed downstairs to Uncle Joey's office in the basement. Mr. Fiore was already there. Uncle Joey had picked him up that morning.

"Everything okay, Desiree?" he asked as I came down the steps.

"I think so." I put the paper work I'd filled out with the sisters down on his desk. "There wasn't anything weird about Mr. Fiore, was there?"

He put his reading glasses on and started going over the paperwork. He was a big man. He filled his desk chair and then some. All bulk when my dad—his brother—had been long and lean. Uncle Joey had gone gray young, which had always made him seem older than he was, but his hair was still thick. If I met him on the street, I might not be able to guess his age. "What kind of weird do you mean?"

I pulled up a chair to his desk. "I don't know. Something out of the ordinary, something not right."

He set the papers down and peered over the top of his glasses at me. "Why do you think there might be something wrong?"

I explained about what I'd overheard. "It sounded like Daisy was accusing Iris of something. Something bad. And Iris didn't exactly deny it."

"Did they say it had to do with their father?" Joey asked.

I thought. "No, but what else would they have been talking about? They were here making arrangements for their father who just died."

"After a long and painful illness," Joey pointed out. "His passing wasn't unexpected."

"I know." I kicked at the floor with my toe. "It felt wrong, though. Maybe not wrong. Just weird. They were all sweet and supportive with each other until I left the room. Then they had this whisper-fight that made it sound like Daisy always thought Iris did things that were wrong. Then they both acted like nothing had happened the second I walked in. Like they were covering something up."

"Or maybe it was something they didn't want to talk to someone outside of the family about." Joey turned back to the paperwork. "You did a good job with these. Very thorough."

"Thanks." I gave him a half smile. Doing good work at a job I didn't want was a step up from failing at a job that I didn't want, but only one step. "When do you want to do the pick up?"

Joey tapped all the papers into place and set them in a file folder, which he then stashed in his desk. He took off the reading glasses and set them on a little tray. He was a very precise man. "Now if you have the time."

We didn't drive the hearse to the hospital. It was a little too conspicuous. We kept that for actual drives to the cemeteries. The van was set up a lot like an ambulance. The back was largely open, but with places where we could secure a gurney so it didn't bounce around in the back as we drove.

We pulled out of the long driveway that led to Turner Family Funeral Home and headed west toward town. Taylor's Pumpkin Patch was open for business. It wasn't crowded on a weekday, but the dirt parking lot would be full come the weekend. People came from all over for Taylor's Pumpkin Patch and the Verbena Corn Maze. They stayed for the Haunted House and the Ghost Tour.

The Ghost Tour had always been a sore spot with Dad. He'd absolutely refused to be part of it despite being begged to be a stop on the tour. He'd said most spirit sightings were the products of grief. People didn't want to believe someone they loved was dead so they found a way to keep part of them alive. He'd felt his job was to help people deal with grief and let go. The whole idea of manufacturing something that would keep someone from processing through their sorrow had been an anathema to him. One year, Tamera Utley, who ran the tour, had brought a group to the foot of our driveway. It was probably the only time that I'd ever heard my father raise his voice in public, with the exception of my volleyball games in high school. Tamera had stood her ground at first, pointing out that she wasn't on Turner property and she could stand wherever she wanted with a group to talk about ghosts. Eventually she'd given up, though. She'd said Dad was putting out negative vibes that were scaring the ghosts away.

Gray clouds gathered west of us in the sky and there was a slight scent of damp in the air. "Do you think it'll rain?" I asked Uncle Joey as he drove at exactly the speed limit through town, hands on the wheel at ten and two.

"I hope not. The corn maze always smells funny if it gets rained on." He wrinkled his nose at the thought. The maze had just gone up. Right now, it gave off a smell an awful lot like freshly mown grass. That could turn fast with much more than a light sprinkle. It was close enough to Turner's to have the smell waft over us if the wind was right.

We pulled into the alley at the back of the hospital. Uncle Joey parked and we slid the gurney out of the back, up the wheelchair ramp, and through the double doors into the back entrance of the hospital to go to the morgue. The squeak in the wheel I'd already greased echoed in the tiled hallway, only partially masked by the buzz of the fluorescent lights overhead. We traveled the short distance to the morgue.

"We're here to pick up Violet Daugherty." I handed the clipboard to the woman behind the desk. Violet had been the office manager at the insurance office where my brother-in-law, Greg, worked and I'd written about her accident for the *Verbena Free Press*. Otherwise, I didn't really know her. She must have moved to Verbena after I left and before I moved back.

The woman looked at the paperwork, nodded, and handed the clipboard back. Then she consulted her computer. "Come on in." She got up from her desk and motioned to us to follow. She found the appropriate drawer for Violet Daugherty and pulled it out. Uncle Joey and I positioned our gurney next to it and made sure the black body bag was in the right spot.

Uncle Joey and I took our places at either end of Ms. Daugherty and shifted her onto our gurney on the count of three. We weren't exactly the most evenly matched transfer team around. Uncle Joey was several inches over six foot. I was quite a few more inches beneath it. We made it work, though. Practice and perfection and all that.

Uncle Joey frowned at Ms. Daugherty's paperwork. "Who's her next of kin that's making the arrangements?"

"A cousin back in Maine," the woman said. "We had a heck of time tracking down who her next of kin was. I guess Ms. Daugherty was kind of on her own. I'm not sure the cousin ever even met her."

"Really?" I couldn't quite imagine that. Then again, my family was kind of tightly wound.

293

"Yeah. You'll have to call her to make arrangements. Oh, yeah. Dr. Nate Johar will be by tomorrow to sign off on the death certificate," she said. "Wasn't he just at your place last week?"

Uncle Joey made a noise in his throat. "Seems like he's always at Turner's these days."

The woman scratched at her head with her pen. "What's up with that?"

Uncle Joey opened his mouth, but I rammed him with the gurney. "I have a service to prepare for back home. We should get moving," I reminded him.

He shot me a look, but he started walking.

The truth was that the ME had been spending a lot of time at Turner Family Funeral Home for the last few months and I was pretty sure it wasn't because we had the best lighting or the newest facilities. I was pretty sure it was because of me. Maybe I'd ask him a favor when he stopped by. Maybe Iris had hurried her father along to his inevitable and imminent demise. I'm sure she wouldn't be the first person to feel it was a mercy to put someone out of their misery, especially if it eased their own suffering as well. Maybe Nate could take a quick look at Mr. Fiore and see if anything looked hinky because something certainly felt hinky.